BELIEVE

Believe

Abby Rosser

WordCrafts

Believe is a work of fiction. All references to persons, places or events are fictitious or used fictitiously.

Believe
Copyright © 2017
Abby Rosser

Cover concept and design by Jonathan Grisham for Grisham Designs, LLC. Author photo by Nancy Center Photography.

Published by WordCrafts Press
Buffalo, Wyoming 82834
www.wordcrafts.net

Contents

DEDICATION

This book is for my four:
Ella, Lucy, Knox, Ezra.

I believe in you.

It is also for Brent,
my favorite person ever.

Thanks for believing in me.

Chapter 1

WELCOME TO PEACOCK VALLEY

Dooley wasn't hiding, not really. In the last few weeks, he often climbed out his bedroom window to sit on the porch roof of his house and *most of the time* it wasn't because his mother was calling for him. On this particular summer morning, he had situated himself on the warm, sticky shingles before he heard her voice, but he knew it would come.

"Dooley, I'm leaving."

He could hear the jingle of keys and his mother's voice as she muttered, "Where's my phone? Oh, here it is. Now... where is...I just had that list..."

Dooley sighed. *This might take a while.* Ever since they had moved to Peacock Valley at the beginning of the summer, she was always in search of some lost item. They

1

still had cardboard boxes in nearly every room, waiting to be emptied and their contents put away.

"I'm going to the grocery store, Dooley…if I can just find my…" Her voice trailed off as she walked in to an interior room, away from any open windows. A moment later, Dooley heard the metallic screeching of the garage door as it slowly opened, and their maroon minivan backed out, turned, and started down the long gravel drive.

"Another boring day in Boring Valley where I will probably die of extreme boredom," Dooley thought. He still hadn't forgiven his father for taking the new job and making them move to Minnesota.

"They want me to be manager!" He remembered his father saying proudly. "Manager of the tasting division of the Peacock Valley Jelly Company! Can you imagine that? Me…a manager!"

Dooley thought *his* day was boring. Most likely his dad's was worse. How could anyone get so excited about jams and jellies?

Dooley hugged his legs and rested his chin on his knees. He stared out at the expansive overgrown field beginning at the edge of the narrow strip of his front yard, stretching all the way to the highway.

The grass was tall and dry. The occasional breeze swept over it in waves. Clumps of scraggly trees banded together in groups of twos and threes near the edges of the five-acre expanse.

In the center of the field grew a lone white ash tree. It was taller than his house, and its branches spread wide and full around it. It appeared far healthier than any other plant-life on the property.

Dooley sighed again, ready to close his eyes and imagine himself back to Boston eating ice cream at Brigham's with his best friends, Tim and Drew, laughing and joking without a care in the world. He wished something would happen that would make this move worthwhile. Some kind of sign to let him know that being in Peacock Valley was a part of a greater plan.

Suddenly, a movement caught his eye. The wind was still. The grass stood tall and motionless with the exception of a curving path of bent grass coming from the adjoining field to the right and snaking toward the ash tree. Dooley wondered if the path was made by a neighbor's cat, searching for an unsuspecting field mouse to pounce on.

As the creature crept nearer to the tree, Dooley realized it was something brown and furry, but it seemed too large to be a cat. He continued to watch its slow, deliberate progress. When it finally reached the tree, it stood about three feet tall on its hind legs and looked with quick, darting glances around it. In a lightning second, it looked straight at Dooley before it disappeared near the base of the tree.

Dooley rubbed his eyes with the heels of his hands. The creature—part oversized beaver, part wart hog—was carrying a small, leather bag with the strap diagonally crossing its chest. Stranger still, Dooley thought it had saluted him with a small, furry paw just before it dove down, out of sight.

Chapter 2

ANY OTHER NAME

Dooley decided he must have been out in the sun too long since his eyes were most definitely playing tricks on him. He climbed back in the house through the window and went downstairs to search out something to eat.

Standing in the cool of the open refrigerator, Dooley realized why his mother needed to go to the grocery store. He saw an open can of peaches, a jar of sweet pickles, half a bottle of apple juice and a container of bologna. The edges of the last two bologna slices nearest the opening of the container looked rubbery, but they passed the smell check. Dooley set the peaches, pickles, juice and bologna out on the counter.

He checked the pantry. His parents' cereals sat on the lower shelf. They had names like "Fiber Nuggets" and "Carob Chunky Chews." Dooley thought he'd rather eat tree bark, which would not be far from the ingredient list on the sides of the boxes.

On the shelf above the cereal, he saw various jars of jelly, all of them wearing the bright purple "Peacock Valley Jelly Company" label. He chose one of the jars, grabbed a bag of sandwich bread with only the heels remaining, and added them to the rest of his feast.

"A Taste of Southeast Asia: Rambutan-Durian," he read aloud from the jar label. "Jellies from Around the World." He remembered his father telling him how the Jelly Company had experimented with exotic fruits just before his arrival as manager. Since this one was on their shelf—unopened and dusty—Dooley wondered if it was because it had failed the taste test and the Jelly Company couldn't sell it in the stores.

Dooley held the small jelly jar up to the kitchen light and examined the creamy blobs inside. He shook the jar vigorously then stopped to watch the blobs swirl and dance. As he was about to open the lid, the doorbell rang.

With one eye closed and the other eye looking through the peephole, Dooley surveyed the boy standing on his front porch. After he had determined it was a boy about his same age and size who posed little threat to him, he opened the door.

"Hello. I live next door. My name is Cyrano, Cyrano Mulligan," the boy said with a sniff.

"Hey. I'm Dooley." Dooley wasn't sure if he should shake Cyrano's hand like his father did whenever he made a new acquaintance. It felt like it had been eons since he'd been around other kids his age, and he couldn't remember how to act. He chose to pass on the handshake. Instead he asked Cyrano if he wanted to come in.

"Sure." Cyrano followed Dooley into the living room and they both sat down in the matching mauve armchairs. Cyrano adjusted his thick eyeglasses as they slipped down his long, slender nose. Then he folded his pale fingers neatly in his lap and sniffed again.

"We moved here from Boston," said Dooley.

"Oh. I've never been to Boston. Is it nice?" asked Cyrano. *Sniff.*

"Oh yeah. It's terrific. There's all kinds of stuff to do. There's Fenway Park and the harbors, and there's a bunch of American History stuff, if you like that sort of thing."

"Well, we don't leave Peacock Valley much." *Sniff. Sniff.*

Dooley was beginning to think Cyrano's sniffing was his way of suggesting that their house smelled bad. Every time Cyrano sniffed, his nostrils flared to create two giant holes in the middle of his face. Dooley thought with a few more, he could use Cyrano's head for a bowling ball.

Suddenly there was a loud pop, followed by the sound of shattering glass. Both boys ran into the kitchen where they were immediately assaulted with a smell that Dooley's mother would later describe as "a skunk with the stomach flu wearing sweaty gym socks *in MY kitchen.*"

The boys covered their faces and ran outside for a breath of clean air. "What was that?" Cyrano asked.

"It was some sort of jelly, gone bad." Dooley coughed. "I'll have to clean it up before my mom gets back."

Dooley couldn't believe it when Cyrano followed him back into the kitchen. Cyrano opened several drawers until he found one with dishtowels. He pulled one out of the drawer, tied it across his mouth and nose like a bank robber and asked, "Where's your broom?"

Dooley found another dishtowel and did the same. They swept up the broken glass and wiped up the jelly the best they could, then they went back outside.

"Can I ask you a question?" Dooley asked once they sat down on the porch steps. "Could you smell the jelly before it exploded?"

"Yes. Except I thought you were going to be attacked by a skunk or something." Cyrano looked down at his hands self-consciously. "It's not a very good power, is it?"

"Power?"

"I mean…if you could have a magical power, any power in the world, would you pick Olfavoyance?"

"Olfa-what?"

"Olfavoyance…*Nose*-tradamus? A *Schnoz*-ard? It's the power to smell the future." He said matter-of-factly. "Not very impressive, is it?"

Dooley's mind was so full of questions, he couldn't decide which one to ask first. "You have a magical power." Dooley said, his voice a mixture of mocking and apprehension. "And it's olfa…olfa…whatever."

"Yep. That's what happens when you have a bunch of older brothers and sisters, and they get all the good powers first."

"So, you all have powers? You know that sounds crazy, right?"

As if he hadn't heard the skepticism in Dooley's question, Cyrano continued, "My brother Cashel has the best one. He's a Carver. He can make animals out of stone and then, the next morning—*poof*—they come alive. It's really amazing."

"Do you actually expect me to believe…" Dooley began.

"And then there's my sister Clio," Cyrano interrupted. "She's a Rhymer, you know, a Spell-Speaker. Her spells are usually terrific…except when they're not. Like the time she tried to write one to clean up the bathroom. It was supposed to end something like: *'Finish with the brush. Then give the toilet a flush.'* But instead she said: *'Finish with the brush. Then give the toilet a gush.'* Water started gushing out of the toilet and all over the floor. Believe you me, it was some kind of a mess. Much worse than what we started with."

"Is this a joke or something? Like maybe you always do this to the new kid in town?"

"Do what?"

"Tell him crazy stuff to see if he'll believe it," answered Dooley.

"No. You're the only person outside our family I've ever told any of this to."

"Why me?"

"My mom told me to come over. She said you're one of us."

"What's that supposed to mean?"

"My mom is a Namer so if she says you have a power then you have a power."

"Well, your mom is even crazier than you 'cause I don't have a magical power. If I did, I would've already used it to get me out of Peacock Valley."

"It doesn't work that way. My mom's always saying, 'Your power is your gift. Use it for others.' She gave each of us our names, and then when we turn eight, she tells us our powers."

"What about your dad? Does he have a power?"

"No. He's an optometrist."

Cyrano began sniffing the air, then he put his finger in his mouth and pointed it up in the breeze, testing the direction of the smells. "Looks like my mom's going to bake oatmeal cookies this afternoon. I'd better get in there to make sure she leaves out the raisins." Cyrano stood and brushed off the seat of his pants. "Come over anytime, Dooley."

"Sure…maybe…I'll see you," Dooley stammered.

He watched Cyrano's loping strides as he walked back to his house. He couldn't necessarily smell his future, but suddenly Dooley didn't think his summer would be so boring after all.

Chapter 3
SIREN SONG

The two days following Dooley's introduction to Cyrano were spent indoors due to fierce thunderstorms. By the afternoon of the second day, Dooley was pacing the length of his bedroom like a caged tiger. He was eager to get outside but nervous he would run into Cyrano. He had finally decided everything Cyrano had told him was a lie, a practical joke.

"No one has magical powers," Dooley muttered to himself as he paced.

Nevertheless, he felt an undeniable pull to their house and to the Mulligan family. His mother knocked on his bedroom door. "Hey, Dooley. May I come in?"

"Yes."

She stooped to pick up a few dirty socks and threw them in the hamper. Then she sat on his bed.

"The rain's starting to let up. Why don't we go in to town? You need out of this house as badly as I do."

"I don't really feel like it."

"I know this move wasn't what you wanted, but we're here and you've got to make the best of it. You have to start making an effort."

Dooley sat down at his desk chair and folded his arms without a reply.

"I don't think you're being fair, Dooley. Small towns have a lot to offer…"

"This is *nothing* like Boston. I'm a thousand miles away from any of my friends and anything fun to do. "

"So you want to compare this to Boston? Fine. Did you have a house with five acres in Boston? No. We had a tiny apartment with the closest park two subway stops away. You'll make friends, Dooley, believe me."

Dooley looked doubtful.

"Come on. Let's go find an ice cream place, but if you say one word about how the ice cream is better in Boston…"

"Okay, okay. I get it."

Dooley and his mom drove to the town square and parked in front of an ice cream parlor called Eddie's. They decided to forego an umbrella and dashed from their van inside the shop.

A girl was standing behind the long metal ice cream freezers. She had her back to them as they entered, but Dooley knew she worked there by the strings of her striped apron and her striped sailor hat. She was humming softly as she listened to the music in her headphones.

Dooley didn't recognize the song, but the sound of the girl's humming washed over him, soothing his worries away. It was as if she were massaging the furrows on his forehead and whispering comforting words in his ear. He suddenly remembered when he was little, and his mother had rocked him after a bad dream. With that memory in mind, Dooley turned to look at his mother, and her face wore the same expression of peace and contentment.

When the girl finally turned around, she stopped humming and took off her headphones. "Oh, I'm sorry. I didn't hear you come in."

When Dooley saw her, he knew immediately she must be related to Cyrano. She had the same dark hair and pale skin. She also wore the same glasses with thick lenses and large, black frames.

"What can I do for you?" she asked, pointing to the variety of ice cream choices in the cardboard canisters. "We've got two new flavors today: Blueberry Buckle and Key Lime Pie. Of course, my favorite will always and forever be Chocolate Supreme."

Dooley felt like he could listen to her talk all day. Her words took on a rhythm, both steady and surprising. They sounded like music notes, climbing up and sliding back down ever so gradually. Her voice sweetened her words until they nearly dripped with syrup.

"Dooley?" His mother's voice brought him back to reality. "Do you know what you want?"

"Oh, I'll just have that one."

He randomly chose the canister just in front of him

without looking. It held frozen, neon pink peaks of ice cream.

"One scoop or two?" asked the girl. Dooley thought he might have heard another voice blended with the girl's, harmony coming from one mouth.

After she had handed over one cone of Chocolate Chip for his mom and one cone of Pretty Pink Princess Party to Dooley, he finally worked up enough courage to ask her if she was a Mulligan.

"Yes. I'm Cicely Mulligan."

"Well, we're your neighbors. I'm Dooley Creed and this is my mom, Rose."

"My brother Cyrano told me about you." Cicely looked at Dooley intently, as if she were searching for something invisible to most people. After a moment she cocked her head and smiled a little. Then her smile grew until her cheeks were high and round, and her eyes were only dark lashes, magnified by her glasses.

"It's nice to meet you, Cicely," Dooley's mom said as she pulled dollar bills out of her wallet.

Cicely handed Dooley's mom her change as another customer entered the shop. "It's nice to meet you, too," said Cicely as she continued to look at Dooley. She gave him one last smile before turning to help the next customer.

After observing that the rain had completely stopped, Dooley and his mom stepped onto the sidewalk outside the shop. The weighty, humid air clung to their skin and clothes, and it even slid into their lungs as they gulped wet breaths. Dooley turned his cone quickly to lick the sides of his melting, pink scoops before the ice cream drops made it to his fingers. In racing the heat that threatened to completely liquefy his ice cream, he devoured it before they reached the van.

Nearly home, Rose spotted a rainbow in the distance. "Look Dooley! You can see both ends!" she exclaimed.

Dooley leaned into the car window, pressing his nose against the glass. He searched for the exact spot where the arch ended.

"Maybe you'll find a pot of gold, me laddie," said his mom in her best imitation of a leprechaun. "Ah, they're always after me Lucky Charms."

Dooley pressed his face even further against the window so his mother couldn't see him smile.

After they had turned in their driveway and pulled into the garage, Dooley hopped out to look at the rainbow again. He could still see the entire curved arch, and he marveled at the size of it.

As he started to walk to the field in front of their house, his mother called, "If you see a pot of gold, I get half. It's only fair since I saw the rainbow first." Dooley shook his head, smiling, and waved her off as he continued to the edge of the yard.

The ground was drenched and sucked at his sneakers with every step. Tall, wet grass brushed against his bare legs, and soon he was soaked from the waist down. Eventually he reached the large tree in the middle of the field. He walked around the base of the tree, running his hand over the rough bark. It was enormous. If his mom and dad held hands with him to make a circle around the tree, their hands wouldn't reach. The tree reminded Dooley of the Giant Sequoias he saw when they visited Yosemite Park last summer—some even wide enough for people to walk through.

When he had made a complete circle, returning to the spot where he had started, Dooley turned to face his house. He stepped backwards to see exactly where he had been sitting on the porch roof on the day of the exploding jelly. When Dooley dropped his foot, his heel met with something squishy, softer even than the wet mud under the tree branches where grass couldn't grow, and he heard a crunching sound amidst the squish.

He was afraid to lift his foot, assuming he would see some flattened, oozing bug. Instead, Dooley found the broken remains of a small basket, crudely made of bark and twigs. A sticky mixture spread from the center. It was an amber-colored goo with bunches of reddish petals mixed throughout. A few inches away from the ruined basket, Dooley saw a berry in the same orangey hue. He reached down to pick up the unscathed fruit. With the exception of its coloring, it looked like a large blackberry with red petals and a long, thin stalk. He held it carefully, considering its delicate design and its ready-to-burst plumpness.

Dooley scraped the gooey mess from the bottom of his shoe with his hand and smeared it on the tree trunk. Then he cleaned off his fingers on his shorts. The aroma from the smashed berries was strong and sweet. Suddenly the smell changed. It took on a burning smell, reminding Dooley of the afternoon he spent at his grandfather's garage burning his initials on the bottom on the small, wooden racecar they had built for his scout badge.

He looked back at part of the tree where he had spread the berries. Gray smoke was rising from the surface while a design was revealed. Letters, then words appeared, burned into the wood before his eyes.

> It takes a spell to break a spell
> A lute
> A flute
> A toot
> May rout the root
> Before dusk's knell
> Save us from this beastly cell

A shiver ran down his neck past his shoulders, and Dooley stumbled backwards. He tripped on one of the lumpy tree roots that had grown too large to stay underground, and he fell into a sitting position in the mud. His hand landed in the smashed berries and crumbled basket. He stood quickly and ran all the way back to his house.

When he entered the kitchen, he realized he was still holding the berry in his cupped hand. He set it on the counter while he washed his hands, uneasily observing his fingers shake under the running water.

"Would you look at this?" Dooley hadn't noticed his father was home, let alone standing next to him at the kitchen sink. "That looks like a *Rubus chamaemorus.*" His father picked up the berry and admired it.

"A what?"

"A *Rubus chamaemorus,* also known as a cloudberry. I've been experimenting with a line of Scandinavian jellies for work and this one's a beaut. Where did you get it?"

"Oh, I found it…out in the field."

"Well, it's unusual to find these around here." His father popped the fruit in his mouth and picked up the plate of raw burgers to take to the patio grill. "I guess this place is just full of surprises."

Chapter 4

UPSIDE-DOWN

The next morning began with sunshine and a cloudless sky. Dooley came downstairs just in time to see his father leaving with a piece of toast in his mouth, a travel mug of coffee in his hand and his briefcase tucked under his arm.

"Hey there, sleepy head," his dad said as he pulled the toast from his mouth. "You ought to try some of this jelly I brought home. It's made from figs!"

It took every ounce of Dooley's willpower to keep him from rolling his eyes. "How can you eat that for breakfast when you know you'll be tasting that stuff all day at work?" asked Dooley.

"Love what you do and do what you love, son." Dooley's supply of willpower was no match this time; his eyes rolled up, sideways, and backwards. Luckily, his dad was out the door without ever noticing.

"So, what are your plans today?" his mother asked.

"I don't know. Probably nothing."

"I'm going to empty the last boxes in the basement. You're welcome to help…"

"Tempting, mom, really tempting."

Dooley poured himself a bowl of cereal. "I think I'll go next door and see what Cyrano's doing."

"Suit yourself."

After breakfast, Dooley walked over to the Mulligan house. He had to maneuver through an obstacle course of bikes, birdbaths and beach balls to get to the front door.

He climbed the steps and pressed the doorbell. He heard no sound from inside the house. Feeling his resolve trickle out of him, Dooley was about to turn and walk back home when he noticed something twitching by his shoe.

A shriveled fern sat in a large pot to the side of the door. All of its fronds spread out in lifeless defeat with the exception of one, which curled slightly at the tip. Slowly, the single frond raised itself until it was level with Dooley's elbow. Then, unexpectedly, it wrapped itself around his wrist.

Dooley tried to pull and pry himself free, but the plant only gripped him tighter. It raised Dooley's arm until his hand brushed against the knocker. Dooley grasped the knocker, and the frond swung his arm back and forth three times. Then it unwound itself from Dooley and slunk back down to the pot, innocent as any dead plant. When Cyrano opened the door, Dooley was still rubbing his wrist.

"I see you've met Jeeves," Cyrano said as he motioned toward the fern. "That was all Calix's idea. I thought we should just fix the doorbell, but she's got a thing for ferns."

Dooley and Cyrano entered the house. "Mom, Dooley's here," Cyrano shouted.

Dooley was surprised how similar the basic floor plan of this house was to his own, but that was where the similarities ended. The walls of the foyer at his house were painted beige, and the banister leading to the upstairs bedrooms was dark wood. At Cyrano's house, every bit of the foyer—walls, trim, steps, even the floor—was painted a deep, robin's egg blue.

To his left, Dooley saw the living room with every inch covered in sea foam green, even the sofa, armchairs and stone fireplace mantle. To his right, he saw the dining room, awash in peachy-pink down to the ten peach chairs around the large, peach table. A peach-colored bowl in the center of the table was full of actual peaches.

"Come on. I'll show you my room," said Cyrano as they climbed the blue stairs.

The blue walls and floor continued all the way up to the hallway. When they reached the top, Cyrano pointed to the closed bedroom doors.

"That's Cashel and Crispin's room. That one's for Cicely and Calix. Clio and Celeste share that one. That one used to be mine—mom and dad said I could have my own room since everybody's smells make me nauseous—but when Granny Gibbs moved in with us, she took their room downstairs and my parents took my room. Eh, who cares? Now I get this."

He pointed to the blue ceiling where there was a wooden, rectangular door with a blue rope hanging from it. He pulled the rope to open the door, and a ladder uncoiled before them. It was made of thick, blue yarn, and it seemed to be forming before their eyes. When it was finished, it looked more like a cruise ship gangway than an attic ladder. Cyrano placed his foot onto the woolen step and placed his hand on the rail. He clambered up the ladder, and Dooley followed.

After he reached the top of the ladder, Dooley understood why Cyrano had been willing to give up his bedroom. His attic room covered the entire top floor of the house. Maps from around the world were hanging on most every wall.

The floor was carpeted with colorful and intricately woven rugs. One was a map of Peacock Valley. One was of a giant tree. The one by Cyrano's bed looked like a family portrait. Dooley felt guilty walking on such amazing artwork. Cyrano sensed his apprehension.

"Don't worry about it, Dooley. Granny Gibbs made these for me. They're pretty much indestructible."

Cyrano kicked off his shoes and stepped onto the map of Peacock Valley. His toes sunk into the thick fibers of the rug. Dooley sat on the edge of the map to remove his shoes then he ran his hand on top of the lush pile. "I can't believe your grandma made these."

"It's her power. You know, she's a Knitter." Cyrano lay on his back with his hands behind his head. "I've always wondered how Granny felt when she found out knitting was her power. It's all well and good for a grandma, but she got her power when she was eight like the rest of us. Kind of disappointing, I bet."

"Yeah, about that... I'm still not so sure about this magical power stuff." Dooley waved his hands in the air like a magician about to pull a rabbit out of a hat.

Cyrano rose up and looked at Dooley. "What do you mean 'magical stuff'?"

"I mean... I don't want to hurt your feelings or anything, but..."

"Okay. Come with me."

Cyrano and Dooley climbed down out of the attic and returned to the upstairs hall. "Let me introduce you to my brother Crispin," said Cyrano as he opened one of the bedroom doors.

The room was divided in half with silver duct tape. In the half to the right of the tape, Dooley saw a pottery wheel and carving tools on a desk in the corner. A muslin sheet covered a round lump on a table. There was gray dust everywhere.

On the side to the left of the tape, every piece of furniture looked to be nailed to the ceiling. The bed, dresser, desk and chair were all upside down. It made Dooley dizzy to look up at them.

"Oh, shoot. He's not in here," said Cyrano.

Just then Dooley saw a pair of shoes on the window glass. They were actually standing on the glass with total disregard for gravity. A dark-haired boy with giant glasses ducked into the room through the open window.

"Crispin, meet Dooley."

"Oh, hey, Dooley." Crispin walked up the wall and onto the ceiling where he sat at a desk, opening and closing drawers. Without looking at them, he asked, "Cy, have you seen my fudge wheel?"

"How is he doing that?" asked Dooley.

"Your what?" Cyrano asked Crispin with obvious delight in Dooley's bewildered expression.

"My fudge wheel." Crispin stood and walked to his dresser. "I'm working on some wingtips, and I've got to mark the welt." He opened and closed more drawers.

"Cyrano, why isn't he falling?" Dooley asked.

"I haven't seen it, Crisp, but it sounds delicious," Cyrano teased.

"A lot of help you are." Crispin strode back to the window and crouched to climb out. "See ya, Dooley!" Then he disappeared.

"Ok, what just happened?" Dooley leaned back against the doorframe for support. "From what I can tell, I either just saw a guy walking on the ceiling looking for a snack or I'm hallucinating."

Cyrano placed a hand on Dooley's shoulder. "Well, you did just see a guy walking on the ceiling—my brother Crispin—but he wasn't looking for a snack. He's a Boots, and he was looking for one of his cobbling tools, at least I think that's what he was looking for. Those tools have got the craziest names."

"So, he makes shoes…that can walk upside down?"

"Yeah, that's how it started. Now he's figured out how to make all kinds of inanimate stuff defy gravity." Cyrano gave Dooley a hearty slap on the back. "All this talk about fudge wheels is making me hungry. You want some lunch?"

Chapter 5

MULLIGAN STEW

The boys headed back downstairs to the all yellow kitchen. Every appliance, the countertops, sink and cabinets were awash in hues of lemon, goldenrod and canary yellow. Cyrano opened the refrigerator and pulled out a container of pasta salad. On his way to the yellow kitchen table, Dooley stepped on a loosely woven, yellow rug on the bright yellow linoleum.

"Watch out, Dooley!" Cyrano yelled.

Before he knew what had happened, Dooley was suspended from the ceiling, ensnared within a yellow net.

"Granny!" Cyrano called. "Come on, Granny. I know you're around here somewhere! I could smell your lavender soap before I came downstairs."

A bent, old woman waddled into the kitchen from the

back door. Despite the heat outside, she was wrapped in a bright shawl made of knitted patchwork squares and wore purple, fingerless gloves.

Dooley also noticed her long, striped socks piling in folds at her ankles. Her wavy, gray hair hung to her waist, and ancient-looking spectacles were perched on her tiny nose.

"Oh, dog-water!" Granny Gibbs swore. She snapped her fingers and the net released Dooley in a crumpled lump on the floor. It instantly regained its rug-like form.

"Granny!" Cyrano groaned. "We have a guest!"

"Well, excuse my manners, son. You wouldn'ta known it was me if it weren't for my smell. That soap of mine always gives me away. The recipe is a family secret, ya know. Anyhow, I was just trying to catch us a Nabber."

"A Nabber?" Dooley asked as he stood, rubbing his sore backside.

"Oh, Granny. You know you're never going to catch anything in that net."

"Don't never tell your Granny 'never,' son." She picked up one of her knitting needles and poked it in Cyrano's general direction. "My daddy told me 'bout them Nabbers when I was a little girl, and he weren't no liar."

"All right, Granny, I'm sorry. Now put those away." Cyrano led her to a yellow chair and helped her sit down. He took the needle from her and returned it to the large basket on the table. "This is my friend, Dooley. He lives next door."

"Dooley, huh? I wondered when you was coming over. I'm Dorothea Gibbs, but you can call me Granny like the rest of them."

"It's nice to meet you." Dooley walked over and sat in the opposite chair.

"Well, what do you think about this place? Not one of your regular kind of families, is it? Yep, this here's a real Mulligan Stew, I tell ya."

"Ma'am?"

"A Mulligan Stew. When my daughter Callidora married Lloyd Mulligan—Lloyd the optometrist," she said, wrinkling her nose in distaste. "That's just what she got: a Mulligan Stew. That's when all the hobos put in something good and cook it all up in a pot to make their dinner. I wasn't too keen on her marrying an optometrist what with all her potential and whatnot, but they've turned out some right good kids with all kinds of powers."

She leaned in toward Dooley, squinting her eyes at him as if he'd just named Cyrano's major flaw. "And I'm not just saying that 'cause I'm their granny."

"No ma'am."

"But I don't need to do no convincing you about them Nabbers, anyhow. Ain't that right, Dooley?"

Cyrano turned from his spot by the open refrigerator door to look at Dooley.

"Who, me?" asked Dooley.

"That's right. You know all about them Nabbers, 'cause you already seen 'em."

"I have?"

"That's so. They're in your tree on your property so by that way of thinking, they're *your* Nabbers. You'd better start investigating on what's gone missing 'cause you can bet whatever it is, you'll find it in that tree."

"Nothing's missing…that I know of…"

"Is she right, Dooley, about you seeing Nabbers…I mean, seeing something unusual by the tree?"

Dooley chuckled uneasily. "Well, sort of. It was just…"

"Was it covered in fur but with a head like a bird or did it have a body like a lizard with the face of a kangaroo? Or maybe it had a beaver tail and big teeth?" Granny asked, excitedly, holding her two pointer fingers against her mouth like tusks.

"I did see something furry…with tusks…and a backpack?"

"Hot diggety!" exclaimed Granny as she slapped her hand on the table. "I knew it! You can see 'em!"

Cyrano shut the refrigerator door and smiled. "Now this is getting interesting!"

Chapter 6

A POET AND DIDN'T KNOW IT

After they finished lunch, Dooley and Cyrano returned to the attic bedroom. "Okay, tell me everything you saw," said Cyrano.

"There's not much to tell, really. In fact, I'm not even sure I saw anything."

Dooley was sitting on the rug with the giant tree in the center. He traced his fingers along a branch until he reached the end then returned to the trunk to trace another one. He looked up to see Cyrano's face, open and expectant.

"Okay, okay. I was sitting on the roof, and I saw a creature, brown and shaggy like a cat but bigger, crawling through the field. When it got to the tree, it looked at me and disappeared."

"So...that's it?" Cyrano sounded disappointed.

"Well, it was carrying this leather bag, and it kinda…well, it looked like it saluted me."

"Like a soldier?"

"Yeah."

"Anything else?"

"Well, yesterday, I went out to the tree and…"

"Cyrano-o-o-o-o!" A voice from the upstairs hallway called to them. "Can I come up?"

"That's my younger sister, Celeste. She's seven and so annoying," he whispered to Dooley. "I have a friend over," he yelled down. "Come back later."

"Cyrano has a friend? Will miracles never end?" another voice asked.

"Ugh. As if one sister in my room wasn't bad enough…" Cyrano's slapped his forehead with his hand.

A moment later, a small girl with two long, black braids hopped through the opening. Her face was covered in freckles, an anomaly from the rest of the Mulligan kids Dooley had seen so far. The freckles on one side of the little girl's nose looked just like the Big Dipper and the freckles on the other side looked like the body and arrow of the constellation Orion.

An older girl followed her into the room. The second girl's hair was just as dark, but it was pulled back into a thick ponytail. Both wore the now familiar Mulligan eyewear.

"This is the one bad part to having my room in the attic: no door for them to knock. Then at least I could say, 'Don't come in' and really mean it," Cyrano said to Dooley.

The younger girl walked directly to Dooley and

introduced herself. "My name is Celeste, and I can talk to animals." She pulled a shivering, white mouse from the bib pocket of her overalls. "Can't I, Clementine?" She stroked it with one hand as she cupped it with the other.

"Anybody can *talk* to animals," Cyrano said. "That's not a power."

"Well, I can *listen* to animals then." She lowered her head so that the mouse's whiskers brushed against her ear. "What's that, Clementine? Really? How very interesting!"

"If animals could talk, they would probably say, 'Put me down and make Celeste go away!'" said Clio.

"*Hmmph!*" Celeste pouted. "Come on, Clementine. Let's go where we're 'ppreciated!" She stomped over to the ladder and climbed down.

"Can she really understand what animals say?" Dooley asked after she was gone.

"I seriously doubt it," said Cyrano. "She won't really know what her power is until she's eight and that's not for another week. She's been telling us she has a different power every month or so since I got mine, and that was almost three years ago."

The girl with the ponytail cleared her throat loudly.

"Oh yeah. Dooley, this is my sister Clio."

"Nice to meet you, boy named Dooley, with crumpled shirt and hair unruly."

"Clio!" Cyrano cried. "Please excuse my sister. She's a Rhymer…"

"A blessing and a curse but a big nose would be worse," she interrupted.

"She's usually not this mean."

Cyrano gave her a cautioning look.

"She's just showing off 'cause you're here."

"Showing off for little boys is not something Clio enjoys." She folded her arms across her chest and stuck her nose up in the air.

"Hey, I'm not a little boy," protested Dooley. "I'm twelve since March. I bet you're not much older..."

"Age is counted by cleverness not years. A boy of twelve may seem a child of his peers."

"She's thirteen," offered Cyrano. She *hmmph*ed just like Celeste and stomped her foot. "The rhyming thing is annoying, but she can't help it."

"Why is that?"

"I don't really know. Maybe it's because she's the one in the family who can write and use spells. It's a pretty cool power but it's actually really difficult."

"Can you do one now?" Dooley asked Clio.

Clio's brow wrinkled as she looked around the room and chewed her thumbnail. Eventually, her eyes lit on a baseball and mitt sitting on the floor below a map of Albania.

Clio took a deep breath and held her hands out, fingers spread wide. She spoke in clear, measured tones. "Spitball, meatball, eyeball, narwhal. Baseball, rise and meet the drywall."

The baseball flew up, hovered in mid-air for a second, and then zoomed toward where Dooley and Cyrano sat. They ducked down and turned just in time to see the ball smash into a poster of Joe DiMaggio on the opposite wall. His large nose was now replaced with the baseball.

"Oh, great! Just what my room was missing: a huge crater in the wall," said Cyrano sarcastically as he jumped up to examine the poster. The area around the ball had caved in making Joe's eyes cross as he looked down at his new nose.

"That was amazing!" Dooley cheered. "Seriously, Clio, you have a fantastic power!"

Clio beamed. "Boys of twelve can be sweet sometimes when girls of thirteen need to say some rhymes."

She kissed him on the cheek and quickly ducked out of the room.

Chapter 7

FUNERAL FOR A DOLLOPBERRY BUSH

When Dooley returned to the Mulligan home the next morning, he was prepared for the defective doorbell. He stood as far from the overly helpful potted fern as possible when he lifted the doorknocker.

"Oh, hello," said a girl in the doorway. She was wearing a large straw hat and gardening gloves. She had sun-blocking lenses attached to the top of her black frame glasses, but with the dark lenses flipped up.

"Hi, I'm a friend of Cyrano's…"

"Oh, yes. It's Dooley, right?"

Her voice was sweet and high-pitched, like softly tinkling wind chimes.

"Yeah."

"I'm Calix. Dear Cyrano is assisting me out in the greenhouse today. Come along, and I'll show you where he is."

Before they descended the front steps, Calix reached in the right pocket of her short apron and pulled out what looked like a pinch of silver dust. She sprinkled the dust on the fern and whispered something to it. It raised one of its long fronds and lovingly rubbed against her leg.

"I don't know if Cyrano told you but I'm a Greenie. My magic powers are revealed through my care and cultivation of plants. Plant life *is* my life, actually. I even dream about plants."

As he listened, Dooley scratched at a mosquito bite, red and swollen on his arm.

"You mustn't scratch it, Dooley. That will only make it worse." Calix reached into her apron pocket and pulled out a tiny plastic bag, closed at the top with a twist tie. It held a glob of yellowish cream. Calix undid the opening and brought out a miniscule dollop of the cream. "Hold still. This may burn a bit." She rubbed it on Dooley's bite. It bubbled then disappeared. "There. Much better. Now, take this." She twisted the bag closed again and gave it to him. "I have more in my room."

"Uh, thanks."

"My pleasure," she answered with a happy sigh then her face grew serious. "I was awoken this morning with the news of Cyrano's troubling premonition. He told me my Dollopberry bushes would expire before nightfall. Well, you can only imagine my dismay…"

Dooley couldn't really imagine her dismay, but he still said, "Oh, yeah…sure…"

"So, we've been working since sunup to save them. My brother's nose really is useful, you know. Luckily, he's familiar with the perishing Dollopberry scent."

"I forgot that one. What does it smell like again?"

"Cotton candy, of course."

"Oh," Dooley had expected something more like road kill or rotten eggs. "That doesn't sound too bad."

"We've been able to save most of the bushes but I'm afraid…I'm afraid for some of them we were too late."

She reached into her left pocket and pulled out a floral handkerchief. She blew her nose and wiped her eyes.

"When you arrived, I had just gone in the house to borrow Cicely's harmonica to play a dignified dirge for the funeral."

She blew her nose again.

The closer they came to the greenhouse, the stronger Dooley smelled a growingly peculiar scent. At first it did smell a bit like cotton candy, but by the time they had reached the greenhouse door, the aroma had changed completely. Now it smelled like the time their freezer had gone out while they were on vacation.

When Dooley and his parents had come home, his mother had been forced to throw away cartons of melted ice cream and bags of thawed chicken nuggets. The combination of sour milk and rancid meat had turned him off eating anything other peanut butter sandwiches for a week. As he opened the door and fully took in the odor coming from the greenhouse, he realized this was much worse.

Cyrano was kneeling beside a row of large, potted bushes with his back to the door. Each plant had a set of thick, pink and yellow branches covered with bright pink circles that looked like suction cups. The droopier plants were also covered in tiny, pink leaves. Using a small pair of scissors, Cyrano was trimming the leaves and catching them in a metal bowl.

"What's he doing?" Dooley asked Calix with the collar of his t-shirt pulled over his nose and mouth.

"He's trying to save my remaining darlings," she whispered. "If he can remove enough of the infected leaves before the plant detonates, then it can be saved. But he must work very carefully. In their present condition, they're as volatile as a stick of dynamite."

They approached Cyrano slowly so as not to startle him. When Cyrano sensed their presence, he turned, and it was Dooley who was startled. Cyrano wore a rubber gas mask with a black tube coming out from the bottom. The glass ovals protecting his eyes were fogged from his breath.

"Dooley?" he said in a muffled voice. He fumbled the scissors and accidentally dropped them with a *clink* in the bowl. Suddenly, the bush he was working on raised its branches as if in surrender and slapped them to the floor, exploding in a cloud of acrid pink and yellow smoke.

Dooley ran out the door, and Cyrano came tumbling out behind him. He peeled off the mask and threw it on the ground.

"Why is it that something ends up reeking anytime you're around?" Dooley sputtered between coughs.

"I was just thinking the same thing about you," Cyrano choked. "Come on. I've got to wash off this smell."

They ran around to the back of the greenhouse to a hand pump. Cyrano primed it with several hearty pumps and then the water began to flow. He rubbed his hands under the waterfall and splashed some on his face.

Dooley sat on a nearby rock, looking toward the Mulligan's wooded backyard. It merged with the property owned by Dooley's family, creating a dense forest.

"How much of the woods is your land?" Dooley asked.

The water had stopped flowing and Cyrano was wiping his glasses on the only dry section of his t-shirt. "Oh, I don't know…not much. Our property is set up like yours, I guess, with most of it in front of the house. The property line back here is somewhere just before you get to Old Homer's cabin."

Dooley felt the hairs on his arm rise and quiver. "Old Homer? Who's that?"

"He was the foreman on the farm that used to make up what's now Peacock Valley. He's about a million years old."

Dooley walked to the edge of the woods and saw a dark outline of a house among the distant trees. "Have you ever met him—Old Homer?"

"Yes, just once. I went to his cabin with my dad a long time ago. My dad wanted to ask him if he would mow the field out front so he could make a Japanese garden or tennis court or something—Homer still has all sorts of farming equipment—but he told us," Cyrano leaned over as if he were using an invisible cane and squinted his eyes.

"'I shan't cut them fields…aye, never! And neither should you, if you know what's good for you!' So we left."

"Did your dad ever cut the field?"

"No. He probably just got interested in something else. He's got tons of hobbies: Tai Chi, tap dancing, topiary pruning, his tea bag collection. He used to be really into making homemade root beer. Right now, his new thing is astronomy." Cyrano replaced his glasses. "My family is really weird, isn't it?"

"Hey, don't worry about it. My dad is obsessed with jelly, so who's to say what's weird?"

Cyrano smiled.

"Speaking of weird…I want to talk to Homer."

"What? Why? He's just a grouchy old guy."

"I feel like he'll have some answers about the creature I saw from the roof."

"Okay but don't get your hopes up too much. Like I said, he's about a million years old."

Cyrano went to tell Calix he would be back later to help her finish up in the greenhouse. When he found her, she was playing "Taps" on the harmonica as she stared down at four Dollopberry bush-sized graves. He decided to leave her to her funeral proceedings and tiptoed away.

Chapter 8

HOMER

The boys entered the woods uneasily. With no well-worn path, they were forced to climb over fallen logs and detangle themselves from prickly branches every few steps. Eventually the trees cleared, and the cabin was in full view. When they reached it, Dooley knocked on the door. After waiting a few seconds, he tried again.

"Are you sure he still lives here?" Dooley asked.

"I don't know. I was only six or seven when I came with my dad. Maybe he's...you know..." Cyrano held an invisible harmonica to his mouth and hummed a few bars of "Taps."

"Yeah...maybe..."

The boys walked around to the back of the cabin. They saw a small paddock holding a lone goat. The animal was mostly cream with a splatter of tan spots on its left backside. It was chewing a mouthful of hay, quietly surveying the boys as its pointed white beard bobbed up and down.

They passed the paddock and walked to the edge of a tidy vegetable garden. Poking out of the dirt at the end of each row were plant markers. Pictures of vegetables were drawn on thin pieces of white plywood and nailed to squat pegs. Dooley recognized peas and cauliflower, beets and radishes, spinach and Brussels sprouts.

They stared beyond the garden toward the thicker forest growth, wondering what the shadows and foliage hid from view. The sudden sound of flapping wings high in the canopy of leaves overhead frightened them and caused both boys to jump. "Come on, Dooley, let's get out of here."

As they turned to leave, they nearly ran into a short, elderly man standing a few feet behind them.

"Why art thou here?" he growled, jabbing at their ribs with his cane. He wore a straw hat with a black ribbon around the band and dark suspenders holding up his loosely hanging, navy trousers. His collarless, cotton shirt was buttoned to the very top. He had no moustache, only a long, white, pointed beard that wagged when he spoke. "Answer me. What right hast thou to trespass on mine property?"

"Sorry, Mister…uh…" Dooley stammered.

"Homer. For 'tis the only name I have 'ere known for these many years, and I shan't be called by any other."

"Well, my name is Dooley Creed. We just moved to Peacock Valley, and I heard you've lived here a while…"

"Long enough to know more'n thee, I'd wager."

"R-r-right, so…" Dooley looked to Cyrano for help.

"So, Dooley saw some strange kind of animal in the field

in front of his house, and he was wondering if you might know what it could be."

Homer narrowed his eyes and insisted, "Speakest thou further of this strange animal."

"Well, it was brown with long teeth like a warthog and it was carrying a leather bag across its chest, and it disappeared by that big tree." Dooley had retold his story frequently enough that now it tumbled out without pause or expression.

Homer's face lost its look of anger and was replaced with a look of wistful longing. "Thou art certain, boy?"

"Yes, sir."

"And this critter…it carried a bag…thou art sure?"

"Yes, sir."

"Hmmm. Thou did not notice he had a peg leg perchance, did ye?"

"A peg leg? No. The grass was too high to see its legs at all."

Homer took off his hat and wiped his forehead with a red bandana. Dooley noticed a mottled design of light brown spots on the left side of his baldhead. Something looked familiar about the spots. They were too large to be freckles and had the appearance of brown paint flicked by an artist's brush. Dooley spun around to look for the goat, but the paddock was empty. When Homer saw Dooley's attention had turned to the vacant paddock, he replaced his hat.

"The sun 'tis high, and ye art thirsty, no doubt. Let us walk thither, and I shalt fetch us drinks."

They walked past the empty paddock and followed

Homer into his cabin. Upon entering, Dooley felt like he was on one of the field trips he had taken with his school back in Boston. They would tour homes set up just like those of early American pioneers and listen to women dressed in period costumes explain how to construct straw brooms and make soap from bacon grease.

A rough-hewn table and chairs sat in one corner and a four-poster bed sat in the opposite corner, covered with a colorful quilt. There was an ancient-looking fireplace bellows leaning against the mantelpiece. Bundles of herbs hung from the rafters.

Cyrano's nostrils flared and narrowed as he checked for possible smells of danger in their immediate future.

"You worried?" Dooley whispered.

"Nah. Everything seems okay. All I'm getting is mold spores, dried burdock root and...*sniff*...peppermint."

Homer set down three metal cups and filled each one with water he dipped from a bucket. Dooley and Cyrano sat at the table, watching Homer's every move and waiting for him to join them.

Homer dropped into one of the chairs and sipped his water.

After a few silent moments, Dooley spoke. "It's obvious you know something about that creature. Can't you tell us what you know?"

Homer looked from Dooley to Cyrano and then back to Dooley again. "The tale I must tell is not for the cowardly nor is it for the sightless."

"I have 20/20 vision with these, thanks," said Cyrano, assuming Homer referred to his thick glasses.

"'Tis not a matter of thine eyes, boy. I speak of thine heart."

"Please, mister…I mean, Homer. Please, go on," said Dooley. He wasn't sure why his heart was pounding as if he had just run a marathon.

"If ye wish…" Homer laid his hands, palms down on the table and drew in a loud, deep breath.

Chapter 9

OLAF THE PEACOCK

"**M**any centuries past, there was a Viking named Olaf, Olaf the Peacock. He was cruel—e'en for a Viking warrior—and as proud in bearing as the vain peacock. His coats were of such colors and magnif-icence he wouldst shame that regal bird, which was his aim.

As Viking leader, his devotion shouldst been his people. Instead, 'twas only his riches and longevity did he give care. As he aged, he searched for naught but a spell to let him live on forever.

"One day, he met a Valkyrie, a beautiful woman of magic and cunning who was given the task of deciding which man shalt die in battle and which shalt live. Her name was Birna. She had admired Olaf for some time and had wanted him for her mate.

She told him he couldst live on for all time if he wouldst

do her bidding, and in swearing an oath she made it so.

Agreeing to her terms, Olaf sealed his fate. She asked for all his children—for he was allowed many wives—to be given unto her. He had fifty-one children in all. He gathered them in the valley on such a day as the Valkyrie appointed with no care for his children's welfare nor future. In the center of this valley stood a giant white ash tree. Its branches reached towards the heavens, and its roots grew towards the land of the dead. Birna flew to the valley on her winged horse and lighted upon that tree.

"Olaf called up to her saying, 'Here art mine children— sons and daughters all—now thou must grant mine wish.' Birna untied the cord from 'round her waist and threw it upon the sons and daughters of Olaf. The cord became a chain and wrapped 'round their ankles, forcing them to be prisoners of this evil witch.

"Birna called unto Olaf, 'Thou hast given these, thy off-spring, of thine own accord so they shalt be mine forever. As for thee, proud Olaf the Peacock, thou wilt be mine also and live forever in mine chamber below the earth.' She spoke some wicked magical words and a door appeared in the trunk of the tree. Olaf was lifted by invisible arms and spirited away into the tree, a prisoner of his own pride and vanity.

"Birna jumped down from her perch on the tree and stood by the children. She said unto them, 'Ye sons and daughters of Olaf, ye art now mine, all one and fifty. I have no children of mine own and ne'er will, as was mine curse.' She counted these children, shivering and scared they were, and they numbered but fifty. 'Who art missing amongst mine children? Who darest not appear before me?'

"The eldest son, Egill, then spoke, 'I know which child of Olaf fails to appear, mine lady. 'Tis my brother Humli.'

"The second eldest child was a daughter named Dúfa. She pleaded with Egill to hush for she loved her brother Humli better than all others combined. Dúfa and Humli shared a kind-hearted and gentle mother. Dúfa had feared her mother's grief would undo her when she learned of Olaf's betrayal, so Dúfa had secreted her younger brother away to keep him safe. 'Humli was killed by the fever last night, mine lady,' said Dúfa. 'He is no more.'

"Dúfa nor Egill knew that Humli didst follow them to the valley but hid in the bushes at the crest of a hill. 'Mine daughter, 'twould be a grave mistake to lie unto a Valkryie. I shalt cast mine spell to secure your allegiance to me for all time. If your words prove false, mine spell will curse all who mine chain holds into empty nothingness.'

"Egill knew Dúfa's words were false, so he set about trying to free himself from the chain at his ankle. He always carried a dagger in his boot, so he retrieved it and sawed upon the chain. Birna laughed at his folly for she knew he would never cut the links as they were forged in the fires of Valhalla. When Egill too saw he would not cut the chain, he began to cut off his own leg—freedom was that dear.

"Birna cried out to him to stop and the other children wept e'en louder. Humli, small but brave, ran from his place of safety and shouted, 'I am here, mine lady. Do not harm mine brothers and sisters!' Egill paused from his bloody task for a moment to see his brother Humli coming near them.

"Birna said, 'Mine children, ye art a naughty brood, and I shan't abide such tricks! I shalt change ye into animals, beastly creatures ye art already, and move this valley to another realm far from thine mothers. Then ye will love me, and I shalt be thine only mother. And thou Humli, bravest of the children of Olaf, thou wilt spend only a portion of everyday as an animal, and that is how I shalt repay thine valor.'

"Birna's speech did naught to stop Egill's dagger. Just as she spoke her ancient and magical words, he cut through the bone, but his task was in vain. For he had naught time to remove the chain and the spell transformed him along with the other forty-nine. Humli looked on with eyes full of tears and witnessed his brothers and sisters in their misery.

"So that is how Peacock Valley came unto this place and the creatures of thine field are prisoners of Olaf's cowardice. They lie dormant for fifty-one years until they art awakened and allowed to roam the valley for a fortnight, before resuming their long slumber once again. Only a human with the power to see couldst view them and their deeds outside of their magical fortress.

"Thou, Dooley Creed, art powerful indeed if thou hast seen these liminal beings. One with such power of sight must also see this is an hour for boldness—boldness not for thine own gain, for the self-seeking shalt never fully see, but boldness in the pursuit of righteousness. For thou wilt surely aid me, and together we shalt rescue mine brothers and sisters from their curse."

Chapter 10

PROPERTY OF AMBROSE E. SULLIVAN

Dooley's mother was thrilled when he brought Cyrano home to spend the night. "We're so glad to have you here!" she exclaimed a little too enthusiastically for Dooley's liking.

"Thank you, Mrs. Creed."

"Is there anything you need—pillow, tooth-brush, blanket?"

"We're good. Mom...seriously."

"Ok, honey. I'll let you know when supper's ready. Oh, Cyrano, you do like meatloaf, don't you?"

"Oh, yes, ma'am."

After they were in his room, Dooley said, "Sorry about my mom. She's just excited because I haven't had any friends over since we moved to Minnesota."

"Don't worry about it. When I asked my mom if I could come over, she went crazy." Cyrano was flipping through a binder of baseball cards he had found on Dooley's desk. "When you're one of seven kids, and your mom homeschools you, and your grandma sets traps for any unsuspecting visitors, and your sister grows monster plants that explode randomly...well, let's just say you don't get many invitations to hang out."

Dooley was on his bed lying on his back, throwing a tennis ball in the air and catching it just before it hit his face. "So...on a scale from one to ten, how completely wacko do you think Homer is?"

"That's a tough one," Cyrano answered as he closed the binder. "It all depends on if you believe that his story is real."

"Do you?"

"Well, it explains that creature you saw."

"I guess..." Dooley continued to throw the ball. Cyrano watched him and waited. "But the only way to know for sure is for us to investigate. If Homer's right, these creatures will go to sleep again soon, and I won't get another chance to see them until I'm like... sixty-three."

"It's been almost a week since you saw it. That doesn't give you much time."

"What do you mean 'you'? Aren't you going with me?"

"Sure, but you're the one with the power to see them, not me." Cyrano answered. "You know, Granny Gibbs' dad was a Visus, too."

"A Visus?"

"Yeah, it's a pretty rare power. You don't run into those very often anymore."

"I don't understand. I've got to be the last person in the

whole state of Minnesota you'd expect to have a special power." Dooley sat up in his bed and tossed the tennis ball back and forth between his hands. "I'm a B/C-student. I'm not good at any sports. I can't play a musical instrument, and nobody wants to hear me sing. I'm so average I might as well be invisible. There's just nothing special about me." He threw the ball on the floor, harder than he meant to. It bounced once and hit Cyrano's leg.

"Ouch."

"Sorry."

"That's okay." Cyrano rubbed his shin. "My mom always says that everybody has a power, something to give. It looks like yours is your vision. Anyway, I don't know why you're complaining. It's a lot better than being a Nose."

"So, I can see stuff that other people can't, so what? If I can't do anything about what I see, what good is it?"

"That may be your main power, but that doesn't mean it's your *only* power. And besides, you've got me and my entire family to help you. If you add up all of our powers, that comes to a pretty amazing *super*-power, actually."

"But I have no idea what I'm supposed to do next."

"When I told Granny I was coming over to your house, she handed me this bag." Cyrano unzipped his duffel and pulled out a knitted tote bag. It was made up of the same colorful stripes as the socks Granny was wearing when she caught Dooley in her trap. "Maybe there's something in here that can help."

Both boys sat on the floor. Cyrano turned the bag upside down and dumped out its contents in a jumble.

Dooley saw an old, brass compass, two links of a black chain, a white feather, a shard from a broken mirror, a pocketknife and a leather-bound journal tied shut with a length of twine. There was an old-fashioned fountain pen slid under twine.

Dooley picked up the journal and carefully untied the twine. He lifted the pen. It felt heavier than he had expected. Opening the journal to the first page, he read aloud, "'Property of Ambrose E. Sullivan.'" He showed the page to Cyrano. "Was that your great grandfather's name?"

"Where? I don't see anything," said Cyrano.

"Right here." Dooley pointed to the page.

"It looks like a blank page to me."

Dooley flipped through the journal, skimming through a flurry of handwritten notes and scribbles, inkblots, drawings and diagrams until he got to the last page. "It's full of stuff, every page." He handed the book to Cyrano, and he did the same thing.

"Nope. I can't see any of it," Cyrano said with a hint of disappointment in his voice.

Dooley took back the journal and flipped to the last page. He read aloud again, "'If you are reading this, then you are a fellow Visus. If I'm still alive, return my journal as soon as possible, you no-good, thieving snake. If I'm dead, then you're welcome to all of the knowledge I've collected about Peacock Valley. I hope it will serve you better than it obviously has served me, if I'm dead, that is. My search for immortality has been plagued by one disaster after another. Dying would be the ultimate failure. Please tell my wife

Rebecca and my little Dorothea that I love them both and I'm sorry. All I wanted was a long life of riches and leisure for them.'"

Dooley looked worried. "So, what happened to your great-grandfather, anyway?"

"All I know is that he died when Granny was little and that he was a Visus. She's always claimed he saw crazy looking creatures in the fields of Peacock Valley, but she never told me anything about his search for immortality."

Dooley looked back at the page. "There's something written here on the side… it's really faint but I think it says, 'Faith is to believe what you do not see; the reward of this faith is to see what you believe.' –St. Augustine"

"That's one of my mom's favorite sayings. Wonder why Ambrose wrote it down in his journal."

"How should I know? He was *your* great-grandfather. It's weird. Some of the letters in the quote are underlined. F, B, D, D, F, B, E…"

"Boys, it's time for supper," Dooley's mom called up the stairs.

Dooley closed the journal and re-tied the twine. "I guess we better get down there. Oh, and let me give you a piece of advice about my mom's meatloaf: you can never have too much ketchup. That is, unless you like to eat meat-fla-vored bricks."

"I don't mind. Your mom is going to bake brownies later tonight." He sniffed the air. "Just make sure you get her to set the kitchen timer…*sniff*…or she's going to burn the whole pan."

Chapter 11

THE MAP

After finishing their ketchup-drowned meatloaf and perfectly baked brownies, the boys went back to Dooley's room to formulate a plan. Dooley took out Ambrose's journal and pen. Then he found a spiral notebook left over from sixth grade. He turned halfway through the notebook until he found a blank page.

"I think I saw a map in here somewhere," said Dooley as he flipped through Ambrose's notes. "Yeah, here it is. I'll write what I see in this notebook so you can see it, too. Then maybe we'll know what we're supposed to do." He set both the notebook and the journal on the floor and lay down on his stomach.

Dooley began writing with the ancient pen. He drew a curved line in the upper left corner. "Here's the Beck River." He added lines to make it wider and squiggly marks to make it look like waves.

"Wait a minute," said Cyrano. "I can't see any river."

Dooley drew a small spiral. "How about that?" he asked.

"Nope. It must be the pen. I guess only a Visus can see it."

Dooley shoved the pen in the back pocket of his shorts. He walked to his desk and rummaged around in the top drawer until he found a pencil. Then he lay back down on the floor. "Okay, I'll try again."

When he had finished, Dooley had drawn a replica of the map in Ambrose's journal. Two inches deep along the edge of the map were tiny triangles they assumed represented woodland areas. The river ran through the upper left corner with a dozen square houses sprinkled around its bends and curves. The center of the map was empty except for one large tree.

"I stink at drawing, so this is pretty bad but in the notebook, this tree is really detailed. Actually, it looks just like that rug in your room."

Cyrano walked to the window. "Which looks just like your tree…right there," he said, pointing to the sturdy ash tree in the front field.

Dooley joined him at the window. He studied the way the light from the setting sun shone through the leaves and branches, casting long shadows across the field. He squinted, searching for movement or an odd patch of color, but he saw nothing unusual.

Cyrano picked up Dooley's map and said, "All this really shows us is that there used to be a lot more trees and a lot fewer houses in Peacock Valley."

"Ambrose did a more detailed section for this part,"

Dooley said as he pointed to the empty circle around the large tree. He turned the page in both books and began drawing in the spiral notebook again. "I think your great grandfather discovered some tunnels." He lightly sketched a large circle in the middle of the page, then he drew a maze of twists and turns inside the circle. He worked slowly, trying to place the various exits and dead ends in the correct places. There were darkly shaded rocks by the end of some tunnels and x's on others. "He must've tried some of these and found out they led nowhere."

"Do you think he was trying to get inside the tree, like Olaf did in Homer's story?" Cyrano asked.

"I guess so. But why would he want to do that?" Dooley looked up from the drawing. "What did Ambrose think he'd find in there? According to his journal, he seemed to be looking for a treasure and something that would make him live forever."

"I think Homer left some stuff out of his story. Maybe he told the whole story to my great grandfather all those years ago hoping he'd help rescue Homer's brothers and sisters, but Ambrose got obsessed with the treasure instead."

Dooley flipped through the pages of the journal again. "This is going to take me forever to get through. What if I don't get all of it read in time?"

"You'll just have to start at the beginning and work your way through. After you get some pages done, I can show them to my family and see what they think. Don't worry, Dooley. We'll help you as much as we can." Cyrano picked up the spiral notebook and took the pencil from Dooley's hand. "On the pages where there aren't any pictures, you can just read it to me, and I'll write it down."

Dooley turned back to the beginning of the journal and leaned against the bed. "Okay. You ready?"

"Yep. Shoot. Just don't read too fast."

Chapter 12

HAPPY BIRTHDAY, AMBROSE

I was a late bloomer; at least that's what Rebecca has always said. I was born in 1899, a year when nothing important happened. I grew up in a family who only read the *Farmers' Almanac* and the clouds. They only spoke when it was necessary and never sang unless they were in church. Come to think of it, I can't recall ever hearing my father even whistle, as some farmers are prone to do.

When I close my eyes and try to return to my childhood, I think of my father and mother and four older brothers sitting around the long table for our meals. I see gray work shirts and denim overalls. I see calloused hands and dirt under fingernails. I see strong backs hunched over a meal of chewy venison and flavorless beans. I hear spoons scraping plates, and I hear chewing and swallowing.

My family never asked for anything more in their lives than what was likely and what had been given to those in the generations before them, but I always knew I was different.

On the morning of my eighth birthday, I woke up in the bed I shared with two of my brothers and looked at the walls of our log cabin loft. It was June, and the chinks between the boards were wide enough to let the rising sun make stripes on my outstretched hand. Slowly, I moved my arm so that it would be striped, too. I played with the light until one of my brothers snored loudly. Then I slipped on my patched overalls and climbed down to the kitchen. My mother was tending the cook stove and frowning.

"Happy birthday, son," she said as I sat down at the table. My father and two oldest brothers had already left for the barn and early morning chores.

Sitting before me was a small object wrapped in newspaper and tied with kitchen string. I untied the string and pulled it out from under the present. Then I wound the string around my thumb and slipped it off, putting the neat coil in my pocket. Wrapped in the newspaper was a pocketknife. It had a bone handle and opened with a smooth click. I knew it was used—probably cast aside by one of my brothers—but it was all mine. I re-wrapped it in the newspaper. Then I hugged my mother around her middle and thanked her.

"Just see that you don't lose it," was all she said.

I ate my biscuits and molasses and went out to do my chores before the summer sun was too high and too hot. I saw my father and brothers as I walked to the barn. "You didn't tie up Elsie last night like I told you to and now she's gone looking for a place to calve," my father growled. He slapped the back of my head hard, and I stumbled forward, almost falling to the ground. "Go and bring her back, Ambrose, or don't worry coming home for dinner."

I ran to the fields, crying and wiping my nose all the way. By noon, I came to the large ash that sits in the middle of the dell. I sat down under its shade and leaned against the tree. I had no notion where Elsie would have run off to, but I knew enough to stay away until my father had sorted out his temper. Speaking aloud but only to the north wind and the warblers roosting high up in the tree, I said, "Happy birthday, Ambrose." I found a dandelion going to seed nearby and picked it. "Make a wish," I said. I shut my eyes and blew as hard as I could. Then I said, "Please make me rich. I want to be rich as a king."

When I opened my eyes, I saw a giant woman standing before me. She had white hair that fell to her ankles. She looked like a queen in her bright purple robe with leopard's fur sewed on her shoulders and around the bottom hem. Though her hair was white, her face was young with no creases or wrinkles. She had a band of gold atop her head with one bright ruby in the center.

"My name is Birna," she said. And she reached her hand down to help me stand. I barely reached her kneecap. She stroked my forehead with one be-ringed finger and said, "Your powers are beyond measure and you will someday see the riches you desire. But you must be content for now."

She pointed toward a thicket of brambles where my little jersey cow Elsie chewed peacefully on a patch of grass. When I turned back, the woman had disappeared. I led Elsie back to the barn and never spoke of Birna to anyone.

On the mornings of my next three birthdays, I went back to the tree to see if Birna would come good on her pledge, but I always returned home, wretched. I would bring the pocketknife and the old scrap of newspaper in my pocket, trying to repeat the events of that first time I'd seen her, but she just wouldn't reappear.

The next year on my twelfth birthday, I returned to the tree. I called out, "Ms. Birna...your Highness...It's me, Ambrose. I'm here for my riches. Remember? You promised."

The only answer I heard was the call of the whippoor-will—lonely and faraway—mocking me. I slid down to the dirt and slumped against the tree. Miserable, I pulled out the pocketknife, still wrapped in the worn-out bit of newspaper. I smoothed the paper on my lap and read the articles, four years old and hardly news anymore. My eyes lit on a story of a bank robbery in Alabama. Eight people were shot dead by a band of outlaws who escaped with $20,000, a king's treasure. I read over the details and tried to imagine what I would do for that much money. Would I kill? Would I steal?

Soon I began to cry. When I looked up, I saw a creature standing before me. It had the body of a tabby cat with the head of a snowy white dove. All along its back it had rows of yellow feathers and a long yellow tail. It rubbed against my leg, purring and cooing, then it spoke, "Do not cry, boy.

'Tis a beautiful day and thou art young." I was taken aback. This otherworldly creature was speaking as a human would!

"Who are you?" I asked.

"I am Dúfa, eldest daughter of Olaf."

Dúfa told me of the curse that brought her and her siblings to this state. She spoke of how her father ransomed them to a powerful woman in return for a long, prosperous life.

I trembled as I asked, "This woman, was her name Birna?"

"Yes," Dúfa answered. "You shouldst not speak to Birna. Thou must promise me this, boy!"

I was never one to listen to advice from others, even magical, talking creatures, so I made no promise. "What happened to your father? Did she grant him his desire?"

"He remains within," she said as she pointed a paw toward the mighty tree where I rested my back. "He lives on and wants for nothing, but he is not free to leave."

"So the tree holds treasure? Gold? Jewels?"

"Boy, thou must abolish all thoughts of Birna from thy mind. It is all folly!"

Soon another creature hobbled to where we sat. This one was covered in brown, shaggy fur. It had a tale like a beaver and a face like a wart hog. One of its legs was replaced with a wooden spike. "Dúfa, who is this? Come away from this boy," it growled.

"Egill, this boy has seen Birna," she said. They looked at each other and exchanged expressions I couldn't understand.

"Hmmph! We have waited one and fifty years for this Roaming. I shan't spend it with a weak and weepy boy," he spat out and waddled away.

I was offended but still resolved to learn what riches were stored inside the towering ash tree.

"Return in the morn, boy," Dúfa purred. "I shall see what is to be done."

I grabbed my knife and wrapped it in the newspaper again. "You promise to be here tomorrow?" I asked.

She nodded her beautiful snow-white head.

"Then I will be back…tomorrow." And I left.

Chapter 13

FERN SEED IN BLOOM

Dooley had been dictating Ambrose's journal to Cyrano for hours and both boys needed a break. It was midnight and Dooley's parents were sound asleep in their room down the hall. The boys crept downstairs to the kitchen to find something to eat. Over glasses of milk and leftover brownies, they discussed what they had learned from the journal so far.

"So we know Ambrose saw the creatures when he was twelve, which would be 1911," Dooley said.

"Right," Cyrano continued. "And the next Roaming wouldn't be until fifty-one years later…in 1962."

"Do you think he lived that long?"

"I doubt it. Mom said Granny was a little girl when Ambrose died. In 1962, Granny would've been in her thirties, not exactly a little girl."

"We're going to have to get more information from your grandma. How much of this do you think she already knows?"

"I'm not sure. She's always called the creatures Nabbers. When I was little, she would say, 'Don't leave that ball in the yard or the Nabbers will get it' or 'I don't know where your other sock is. I reckon the Nabbers got it.' Stuff like that."

"Did things ever go missing?"

"Not that I know of. I just thought she said that stuff to get us to mind her…you know, like 'The boogeyman'll get you if you don't eat your vegetables.'"

Dooley opened the journal looking for the piece of string he had used as a bookmark. He read silently for a moment.

"Okay, listen to this," he said.

Dúfa once told me of the secret powers of the fern seed in bloom. Anyone who can witness a fern flower opening on a summer night will see a swarm of pixies. They will lead the bearer of the bloom to unimaginable riches. If I can but find this bloom, I know it will reveal the location of the tree's entrance.

Dúfa yawned and rubbed her beautiful bird-like eyes as we spoke that day. If only I had known that would be the last time I would ever see her. "Sleep comes after the longest day," she had said, but I didn't grasp her coded words. She had made two requests of me. I attempted one but accomplished neither. Now she is back asleep with her brothers and sisters, and I won't be able to see her again until I'm an old man.

The boys sat in weighted silence until Cyrano spoke. "So, what were the two things Dúfa asked him to do?"

"I don't know. It doesn't say. It only says that he didn't do them."

Dooley looked back at the journal again. The margins around the passage were decorated with pictures of tropical-looking flowers and fairy creatures that were half woman, half hummingbird. The bottom of the page was filled with roots, curling and sprawling to the corners. He thought of the words that had burned on the tree in the place where he had spread the smashed berries nearly a week ago. He tried to remember the message: something about breaking a spell, a flute, and the roots of the tree. Words and images swam in his head, floating by without any order or sense.

He turned the page. "This looks like a list," he told Cyrano. "At the top, it says 'Do Not Forget.'"

"That sounds important," Cyrano replied. "What's on the list?"

- Always travel SE
- Never touch the ground!
- Two links are better than one
- A feather from a Trumpeter Swan will mask your scent
- Look before you leave
- Blindfold
- Wristwatch
- Tin whistle
- Remember Home

"I guess we'll need to collect the stuff on the list before we go exploring in your field," said Cyrano.

"He didn't mention the pocket knife, but I think we should bring it anyway. I'm not sure how we'll defend ourselves against Birna, the all-powerful Valkyrie, with a tin whistle."

"So, you think Birna will try to hurt us?" Cyrano gulped.

"I don't know. I just want to be prepared for anything."

Dooley continued to flip through the pages of the journal. As he stopped to take a drink from his glass of milk, he looked at Cyrano, dozing with his chin resting on his fist. Dooley felt a surge of affection for his new friend. Now that they had this common quest, he felt as if they'd always known each other.

"Cyrano," he whispered, nudging his elbow lightly.

Cyrano woke with a grunt.

"Come on. We'll look at this some more tomorrow."

As they left the kitchen to ascend the stairs, Dooley passed the calendar his mother kept on the wall by the phone. He noticed tiny red letters in one of the boxes:

SUMMER SOLSTICE

It was only a few days away.

An idea, nearly weightless and most likely unimportant, tickled his thoughts until it grew into an itching. Dooley remembered the drawings of flowers and pixies. He pictured Homer's story with its giant woman and hybrid beasts, a hand frantically sawing a leg bone and a different hand hurling a magic curse on a cowering group of children. He attempted to work all of these thoughts into some sort of organization and then fit them in the tiny box on the calendar.

Dooley shook his head, blinking. Sleep was what he needed to solve this puzzle. Sleep and maybe a tin whistle.

Chapter 14

CARVED FROM STONE

After breakfast, Dooley walked with Cyrano to his house. They went directly to his bedroom to continue with the dictation of Ambrose's journal.

"Here's an interesting entry," Dooley said. "Get this one in the notebook."

Tonight, I sat in the rocker by the RCA trying not to laugh too loudly at Jack Benny while holding little Dorothea as she slept in my arms. After the radio show ended, another program came on, and a song called "If I'm not at the Roll-Call, Kiss My Mother Goodbye" began to play. Though the lyrics were meant to be about soldiers in the Great War, my mind was instantly sent to a golden afternoon I spent with Dúfa.

She told me the children were lined up and counted at dawn of every day of the Roaming. She said Birna insisted Olaf line them up in their underground rooms and count all fifty of them to be sure they were present—something Birna said he should've done the day of the Curse. Dúfa told me that morning had been difficult because Egill, her oldest brother, had not presented himself in line with the others. He had bragged the night before that he could fool his father because Olaf's eyesight was failing more with every passing year. Though his eyes were weak, his mind was strong, and Olaf had no trouble counting to fifty.

When he realized that Egill was gone, he flew into a rage and called Birna to punish his son for such willful disobedience. As Dúfa and I chatted, Egill crawled to the grassy patch where we sat. He was bruised and beaten almost to death. Dúfa wept over his matted fur, streaked with blood and dirt. As she cleaned his wounds, she sang a song to him.

The only lines I remember went something like this: "I cry for your mother and mine. I cry for the years we miss. I ask only thou shouldst join us in the line. Why must thou goad father to this?" She told Egill that only a creature like them could fool Olaf at the roll call but there were no others to be used as substitutes.

Cyrano finished writing the section and looked up at Dooley. "Hey," Cyrano said, "I've got an idea."

He jumped up from the rug where he had been writing and disappeared from his room. Dooley followed and found him in the bedroom shared by Cashel and Crispin.

Cyrano's oldest brother was sitting at a dusty desk chipping away at a large chunk of limestone. He wore safety goggles over his regular glasses and a smock with a variety of tools hanging on the loops sewn across the top.

Dooley could see the rudimentary outline of front paws drawn up against a small chest and a swish of a tail in the back. Cashel was carefully hollowing out the insides of alert, pointed ears on the top.

"Whatchya making, Cash?" Cyrano asked.

"A raccoon," he answered without looking up.

"Well, what would you think about making it half raccoon and half…pelican or maybe Gila monster?"

"What?" Cashel removed his goggles and looked at the boys.

"Here's the deal." Cyrano gave a quick account of Ambrose's journal and their conversation with Homer. "So, we need some creatures to trick Olaf. That way we can use some of the real creatures—his sons and daughters—to be our guides and then we can help them escape."

All three boys were silent with Cyrano and Dooley barely breathing. Dooley expected Cashel to tell them they were crazy or at least laugh in their faces, but this was the home of the Magical Mulligan Stew. Anything was possible.

"I don't know if this will work, guys." Cashel scratched his head and a shower of gray dust fell onto his shoulders. "My statues will come to life, but they won't be able to speak or act like the creatures you're talking about."

"Hopefully, that will be enough to buy us the time we need," said Dooley.

Cyrano added, "You wouldn't have to make fifty, just a few."

"Cy, have you told Mom and Dad about your plan? I don't know what they'll say about you doing this."

"I was putting off talking to them about it, but I guess it's now or never."

"Talk to Mom first. If she says it's okay, then I'll try to come up with something."

Cyrano and Dooley went downstairs and found Mrs. Mulligan in the dining room pressing blooms in between the pages of several large books. One of her bare feet was tucked beneath her, and her other foot swung back and forth under the table. Absentmindedly, she played with a slender, silver whistle that hung from a thick chain. Although Dooley had visited their house a couple of times, this was the first time he had actually seen Cyrano's mother.

"Well, if it isn't Dooley Creed!" she said with a smile. Callidora Mulligan was a tiny woman with pale, blue eyes and nearly translucent lashes. Her long blond hair was loosely braided and pulled over her shoulder. She wore no glasses and very little makeup. She looked like a teenager, not a mother to a house-full of them. Dooley was surprised how different she looked from all of her children.

"Mom, we need some advice," Cyrano began. He went on to explain about the creatures and Homer's story. Dooley interjected with bits of information they had learned from Ambrose's journal.

"And whatever we do, we have to put our plan into action soon," added Cyrano.

"Summer solstice!" exclaimed Dooley. "Of course!"

Cyrano turned to look at his friend. "What?"

"Don't you see?" A fog was lifting from Dooley's mind. Pieces were sliding into place. "'Sleep comes after the longest day.' That's what Dúfa told Ambrose. Summer Solstice is the day with the most daylight of the year and it's the day after tomorrow. If we wait much longer, it'll be too late."

Cyrano returned his gaze to his mother. "So, what do you think, Mom? Can we do it?"

Callidora paused then replied, "Dooley...the dark hero."

"Pardon?" asked Dooley.

"Your name...it fits you." She closed the heavy book with a loud, definitive thud. "You're an unlikely hero, Dooley, and in my experience, those are always the best kind. But to be an epic hero of triumph and valor, you must be prepared. We have work to do."

Chapter 15

THE BANNER OF DIVINATION

Callidora checked the time on her slender, golden wristwatch, nodded to herself and placed the whistle to her lips. She blew a sequence of notes—*who-oo, who-oo, whooo*—then she stood with her hands on her hips, expectantly. Moments later Dooley heard heavy footsteps coming from the stairs and hallway. The back door opened and slammed shut. Then Dooley saw all the Mulligan children standing before him.

They stood in birth order; their close proximity to one another highlighted the strong genetic makeup of the kids. Dooley looked them over from oldest to youngest: Cashel brushed gray dust from his hands. Cicely removed her headphones and let them rest around the back of her neck. Calix flipped up the sun-blocking lenses from her regular glasses. She set a watering can on the floor beside her twin brother Crispin, as he sharpened a cobbling tool on the leather strap hanging from his apron. Clio smiled shyly at Dooley and gave him a slight wave. Dooley blushed and returned her wave self-consciously. Cyrano looked from his sister to his friend and rolled his eyes. He was about to comment to Dooley about Clio's goo-goo eyes for him when Celeste tugged Dooley's shirttail. He leaned down to let her whisper in his ear.

"Dooley," she said, "It's almost my birthday."

"Not now, Celeste," Cyrano muttered. "We've got important things to talk about."

"But when I have my birthday, I'll get my power," she replied, defensively. "Then I can help too." She pulled Dooley back towards her and whispered, "Don't tell anybody but I think my power is…invisibility." She opened her eyes wide and raised her dark eyebrows.

"Your birthday *is* coming up, love." Callidora kissed her youngest daughter's forehead. "And we'll need everyone's powers for this. Has anyone seen Granny?"

"She was in the yard a minute ago," Crispin said. "I'll go find her." He ran out of the room.

"What is it, Mom?" asked Cicely, her voice sounded like notes plucked on a harp. "What's happened?"

"I'll let Dooley explain our mission when Crispin comes back with Granny."

No one spoke for a full minute. The only sound came from throats being cleared and restless feet rustling the peach-colored dining room rug. Dooley reached a hand to his hairline to wipe away a trickle of sweat. He began to feel the absurdity of the situation. He suddenly regretted everything he had done and said in the past week, beginning with climbing out his bedroom window to sit on the roof.

Dooley was about to tell them to forget the whole thing and throw Ambrose's journal on the floor and run out the front door and keep on running until he was back in Boston, back in his old apartment in his old room lying on his old bed, when Callidora Mulligan laid a tiny, soft hand on his shoulder.

"You know you're not alone, Dooley," she said.

"But I'm asking you to believe something that sounds so, so…unbelievable. No matter what, you'll still have to just take my word for all of this because I'm the only one who can see anything."

"Do *you* believe?"

Dooley searched for an answer. "Do *I* believe? In cursed creatures and a giant magical woman and a tree with secret tunnels and a Viking warlord trapped inside?" He paused. "Yeah. I do believe it."

"So, you've seen these things and you believe. Okay. Now we won't be able to see everything you can see, but we'll have faith—faith in you."

"Why? Why would you have faith in me?" He looked at the faces of the family now circled around him.

"Dooley, we've been raised on this stuff," said Cashel. "Powers and unseen forces and things that seem impossible."

"Invisibility…" Celeste added, nodding to Dooley.

"And we have always been told that by ourselves we have

the strength of one," said Calix, as she drew a thin branch from her gardening apron. She broke it easily. "But we are stronger when we unite." She held three branches together and attempted to break them. When they couldn't be broken, she reached for the string that hung from Ambrose's journal. She slid it from the book and wrapped it around the bundle of sticks. "Together."

"Remember," added Callidora. "'Faith is to believe what you do not see; the reward of this faith is to see what you believe.'"

As Calix handed the bundle to him, Dooley was about to ask where he'd heard that saying, but Crispin returned with Granny. She was huffing from the heat and exertion, but her face was lit up with excitement. Gray hairs stood up all over her head and her knitted shawl was askew. "I knew it!" she was saying before she was fully in the room. "I just knew it was true!"

Granny waddled over to one of the dining room chairs and sat down with a thump. She dropped her knitting basket on the table and rearranged her shawl. Crispin entered next, dragging something log-shaped and heavy behind him. "Right there, Crispin-dearie, set it right there by Dooley." It looked like a small rug. It was rolled up, wrapped in plain, brown cloth and tied with wide strips of braided fabric.

Granny hummed softly. As she rummaged around in her basket, a ball of yarn was pushed out and rolled the length of the table. Soon she withdrew a long, knitting needle. When she waved the needle at the rug, the strips untied themselves and fell away. Crispin stepped forward to unroll the parcel, but Granny stopped him. "No, dearie. Dooley must see it first."

"Who? Me?"

"Yes, hon." She waved him to step closer. "Dooley, I come from a long line of Knitters. My mother was a Knitter and so was her mother. This banner has been passed down from generation to generation. I've never opened it though 'cause it's no good unless there's a Visus there to see what's on it."

"Granny, you never told us you had a Banner of Divination!" exclaimed Cicely.

"It weren't no use to any of us…'til now," Granny answered. "Dooley, this banner is made from the finest threads in the world. It's ancient, but it's whiter than if it were weaved this morning from the wool of the snowiest lamb. When you open it, the rest of us will all see a blank banner, nothing at all. But when you look at it, you'll see a divination, a prophecy of the future. It'll guide you."

Dooley laid the knitted tote bag he used to hold the journal and the spiral notebook on the table. He lowered himself down to his knees and laid his hands on top of the banner. It felt solid and oddly warm beneath his fingers. After taking a deep breath, he gave the roll a push and watched it unfurl until it hit the wall. He sat back on his heels to take in the entire scene in one view.

"What is it, Dooley? What do you see?" asked Cyrano when he couldn't wait any longer. He knelt beside his friend.

"It's the tree. The leaves at the top…" Dooley motioned to top of the banner. "Are on fire. Then, down here…" He waved his hand at the lower, right area. "In the underground tunnels, there are people and smoke. Their faces look… scared. They're trapped." Dooley looked at Cyrano and saw his own reflection is Cyrano's glasses.

"Where are you? Can you see yourself in the picture?" Cyrano asked.

"Right here." Dooley pointed near the bottom edge of the banner, in the center just above where the roots began to spread and curl. "I'm holding something that looks like a jar and a knife. There's a blue, glowing ball in front of me." He swallowed. "I'm alone."

Chapter 16

THE PLAN

"That's it, Dooley," said Cyrano. "You can't go through with this. A tree on fire? People trapped in tunnels? No way. I won't let you."

"Granny, is this the only future that can be known? I mean, can it be changed from what is shown?" asked Clio. She seemed as nervous as Cyrano.

Granny and Callidora looked at each other. "The banner shows what the banner shows, dearie," answered Granny.

"What's that supposed to mean?" asked Cyrano.

"Granny means that what Dooley sees on the banner is what will happen." Callidora explained. "We don't know when or how or what will happen next or just before, but it *is* the future."

"Not if he doesn't go," said Cyrano. "Dooley, maybe if you just stay in your house all day or you go out of town—way out of town, then maybe none of this will happen."

"But what if the fire and the trapped people still happen even if I stay away? I can't take that risk."

"Risk? You can't take the risk? What about the risk you'll be taking by going in there?" Cyrano fumed.

"Cyrano…" Callidora began.

"No, this is crazy, mom!" yelled Cyrano. "Dooley, I'm going right over to your house and I'm going to tell your parents."

"They'll never believe you," said Dooley. Cyrano turned and walked out the dining room toward the front door. Dooley ran ahead and blocked his way. "Please, Cyrano, I need your help. I need you to tell me when you smell danger. Listen. For the first time ever, I feel as if this is what I'm meant to do, like I'm doing something that matters. But I'm still scared. If you don't want to go in the tree with me, I'll understand, but I need you to help me plan. Help me remember everything we've read and heard and talked about. Please…"

Cyrano's nostrils flared as he inhaled deeply. He took off his glasses and rubbed them with his t-shirt. After he had replaced them, he reluctantly answered, "Okay, okay." He shook his head. "If you're going to go through with this insane plan…I'm in."

The family watched as Dooley and Cyrano rolled the banner and retied the strips. Then they sat in the chairs near Granny. Dooley opened the spiral notebook and looked over his notes. The rest of the family responded to Dooley's acceptance of this mission by joining them at the table.

"So, here's what we know we need," said Dooley. "We'll need some decoy animals for the roll call at dawn."

"I'm on it," replied Cashel.

"Great." He made a checkmark. "And there's something in here about a fern seed in bloom."

Calix sat up straight in her dining room chair. "A fern seed?"

"Yes. It says that if you see a fern seed bloom on a summer night, you'll see a bunch of pixies and they'll show you where to find treasure. Ambrose seemed to think they'd lead him to some sort of door in the tree."

"Well, my greatest wish is to become a pteridologist," said Calix.

"That's a fern expert," Cyrano whispered to Dooley. "I told you she has a thing for ferns."

"But I have never seen a fern with flowers. I don't think it is even possible." Calix stood up and pushed in her chair. "I will go do some research. No need to worry, Dooley. I will not fail you!" She glided out of the room.

"Ambrose left us a list." Dooley turned the pages of the notebook. "We've already got some of this stuff," Dooley continued. "'Always go southeast. Two links are better than one. A feather from a Trumpeter Swan will mask your scent.'"

Cyrano said, "Thanks to Granny, we have a compass, two pieces from an old chain and a swan feather."

"We also need a blindfold, a wristwatch and a tin whistle," Dooley read.

"I have something else I'd like you to bring with you," Granny said as she reached inside her basket and pulled out a metal rectangle the size of a deck of playing cards.

She held it for a moment then opened it to reveal two picture frames, hinged together at their sides. "Dooley, meet Ambrose and Rebecca Sullivan, my mother and daddy." She handed the black-and-white photographs to him.

One photograph showed a young couple, sitting side-by-side to pose for a professional portrait. The woman had Granny's high cheekbones and dark eyes. She had dark hair piled on top of her head and tiny pearls dangling from her ears. She looked away from the camera, down at the floor. The man's hair was light and parted in the middle. He wore a dark suit over a white shirt with a rounded collar. His gaze was direct. He stared almost defiantly at the camera. His jaw was clenched. Neither of them smiled.

The other photograph was a grainy picture of a young boy, around Dooley's age, wearing overalls with rolled pants legs and holding a small puppy. It was a candid shot and blurry with a grove of trees in the background.

"It only seems right that my daddy go with you."

"I'll bring it back to you, Granny. I promise."

"You can use this for a blindfold." Celeste untied the purple handkerchief she used as a headband and gave it to Dooley. "See, Cyrano. I told you I could help."

"And you can take my watch," said Callidora.

"What about your whistle, Mom?" Cyrano asked.

"It says you need a tin whistle, right?" asked Cicely. "Those are different from Mom's whistle. They're more like a flute. You should be able to play a tune on it."

"A tune?" Dooley asked. "I'm not very musical."

"It's not hard to play. I'll get one from my room." Cicely left.

"So what else is on the list?" asked Crispin.

"It also says: 'Remember home, never touch the ground and look before you leave.'"

"I can help with the 'never touch the ground' part," said Crispin. "What's your shoe size, Dooley?"

"Ten."

"Got it. Are you okay with a nice pair of suede moccasins?"

"Uh, sure."

"I'm on it."

"And I'm going to get started on the sculptures. Any ideas of animal combinations?" asked Cashel.

"Do one that's got the head of a dove and the body of a yellow cat. And the other one, make it with the head of a warthog and the body of a beaver."

"Whatever you say, boss."

"Oh, and Cashel…"

"Yeah?"

"Give the warthog/beaver a peg leg."

Cashel and Crispin went upstairs, too.

"So what would you need to remember home and look before you leave?" asked Cyrano.

"I guess I could collect some stuff from around my house that would make me think of home. I'm not sure of exactly what that would be…"

"What else is in the bag from Granny? Maybe there's something we're missing."

Dooley pulled out the compass, the links of a black chain and the feather and put them in one pile. He slid the pen from his back pocket and laid it on the table next to the pocketknife. That left the piece of broken mirror.

Dooley held the mirror up to let it catch the light of the room. It had two smooth, finished sides that met at a corner. The other side was jagged and razor sharp and about the length of his hand. The back was silver and unreflective. He looked at the mirror side, noticing tiny, black spots scattered along the edges.

He expected to see his reflection, a portion of his face. Instead he saw a room: gold and cream patterned wallpaper and a crimson couch, a delicate-looking wooden end table with a marble top. The glass kerosene lamp sitting on the table gave off a faint glow. He glanced behind himself, but those pieces of furniture weren't peach-colored therefore they weren't a part of the Mulligan dining room.

"What the…"

"What do you see, Dooley?" asked Cyrano.

"It's a different room. It's dark so it's hard to see…"

Just then a face passed before the mirror. Gray skin and a thick, red beard. A purple cape was draped over powerful shoulders. Dooley gasped. Instantly and without a doubt, he knew he was looking at Olaf the Peacock.

Chapter 17

LOSING THE FARM

It was lunchtime, but Dooley's buzzing thoughts prevented him from noticing how hungry he actually felt. The dining room was empty of everyone except Dooley and Granny. He continued to jot down ideas in his notebook and re-read passages of Ambrose's journal, all while keeping a constant eye on the mirror.

As he made his way to the end of the journal, he began to notice less writing and more drawings. There were pictures of gnarled and twisted tree roots that transformed into gnarled and twisted fingers as they crept down the margins. Dooley saw every kind of animal, and each had its own pair of wings. Several pages were filled with hundreds of eyes, some human, some cat-like and some reptile. Dooley shivered slightly.

Granny sat beside Dooley, her knitting needles clicking

continuously. She glanced at him from time to time without slowing her nonstop knitting.

"Granny, can I ask you a question?" he asked timidly.

"Sure, hon. What's on your mind?"

"I hope this doesn't make you, um…sad or anything, but I feel like I just have to know…that is, if you don't mind talking about it…"

"Spit it out, son."

"How did your dad die?"

Granny finally stopped her knitting and laid her needles in her lap. She closed her eyes and sat very still. Dooley began to wonder if she'd fallen asleep.

Finally, she spoke.

"When I was only about five years old, a man came to our farm. He was wearing a gray suit and a gray hat and a gray tie and he drove up in a long gray car. He was buying up all the farming land in Peacock Valley. He wanted to cut it up for neighborhoods. My Daddy's brothers had already sold their lots and left town, but Daddy was determined to stay. He had ten acres and he wasn't budgin'. But the man had a letter showing how Daddy hadn't paid his taxes on the farm and the government was going to make us leave whether he sold his lot or not.

"After the man left, my daddy fell to pieces. He started pacing and talking to himself. For days he wouldn't leave the house. Then one day when Mother was out, he pulled me aside and gave me an old shoebox. Inside was all the things I gave you. He told me to keep it safe and never show it to Mother. Then he left."

Dooley waited for her to continue but she only sat, staring at her hands in her lap.

"And he never came back?"

"He told me to be a good girl and he patted my head. He said he'd fix all our troubles or die trying. Then he was gone."

"What did your mother do?"

"Oh, Mother was angry. When I told her that he had left, she dropped her bag of groceries and ran off straight to that ash tree. Of course, Daddy wasn't there, but she found his journal and his ink pen on the ground. Mother yelled and frightened away all the birds then she marched right back into the house. When she got inside, she threw the journal in the wastebasket like it was just a piece of garbage. I fished it out when she wasn't looking and kept it all these years."

"Did she end up selling the land?"

"Yes. She had to. We had no money to speak of, and those taxes were high. She sold the land, and we went to live with my aunt in St. Paul."

"So, when did you come back to Peacock Valley?"

"It wasn't until Callie and Lloyd moved here after they got married. When Lloyd got done with optometry school, they looked all over Minnesota to find a place with no eye doctors. Peacock Valley was on their list. They thought it looked quiet and slow-paced, so they moved here. I came to visit them when Cashel was born, and I knew right away it was my family's homestead. Strange as it sounds, it felt like my Daddy was here with me."

"So that's when you moved here?"

"Not 'til my husband Raymond died a few years back."

"I've never heard you talk about your husband before. Did he have a power?"

"Oh yes, he certainly did. He was a Greenie like Calix."

"Did he grow exploding dollopberry bushes, too?"

"Not that I recall. But…oh, Dooley. My Raymond could tame climbing vines to grow on nothing but air. With a flick of his spade he could set the maple seeds to gather and rearrange themselves into a giant, spinning tornado. His dream, though, was to grow the perfect rose. He had all different breeds, but his favorite was a pink one he called 'Dorothea' after me. He brought me roses every day, dozens of them. He was a wonderful and caring man, Dooley."

"I wish I could've met him."

"People come in and out of our lives for a reason." She reached out her tiny wrinkled hand and laid it on Dooley's. "And we're all so glad you're in ours right now."

"Lunch is ready," Callidora called.

"You'd better go on and eat. Considering what's coming your way, you're gonna need all the strength you can muster."

Chapter 18

IT TAKES A SPELL

The afternoon sped past Dooley and the Mulligan family. Cicely attempted to teach him how to play "Three Blind Mice" on her wooden recorder, despite constant interruptions from the others.

Fifteen minutes into the lesson, Crispin ran downstairs, lifted Dooley's foot to measure it with his Brannock device and ran back upstairs without a word. A half-hour later, Cashel brought down various sketches of hybrid creatures for Dooley's approval before he began to carve them. Just as Cashel left the dining room, Granny came in with her yellow measuring tape to determine the length of Dooley's arms and the width of his chest. She left the room singing, "She cut off their tails with a carving knife…" All the while, Cyrano sat against the wall in the corner of the room flipping through the pages of the spiral notebook.

"Hey, Dooley."

Dooley stopped playing and answered, "Yeah."

"There's a quote here…it's the one my mom always says."

Dooley and Celeste walked over to Cyrano as he read: "'Faith is to believe what you do not see. The reward of this faith is to see what you believe.'"

"Yeah. So what?"

"It's just weird because my mom's been saying it my whole life. Maybe Ambrose taught it to Granny, and Granny taught it to Mom."

"That makes sense," said Dooley.

"Why did you underline some of the letters?" Cyrano asked.

Dooley took a closer look. "That's how it looked in the journal. He had underlined the letters: F, B, D, D, F, B, E."

"Dooley," Cicely almost whispered. "'Those are music notes." She held the recorder to her mouth and slowly played the seven notes.

"Teach me," said Dooley. "That's got to be some sort of clue."

Cicely patiently modeled the fingering and breathing techniques until Dooley felt confident with the short melody.

"I think you've got it," she said. "I'm not sure what you'll do with it, but it seems important. Just don't forget to take your thumb off when you play the D-note."

"Dooley?" said Cyrano. "Hey, Dooley!" Cyrano waved his hand in front of Dooley's glazed-over eyes.

"Oh, sorry." Dooley realized a little too late that he was swaying ever so slightly and staring at Cicely with intensity. He tried to avoid falling under the spell of Cicely's voice, but it was difficult. While she spoke this time, he heard lapping waves on quiet beach with the occasional cry of a seagull. "I don't know how you do that with your voice but it's amazing."

"I found it!" yelled Calix as she tumbled into the room. "I found the fern seed in bloom! *Kara blaberius*! It was so obvious!" She dropped an ancient-looking textbook on the table. "It's not a real fern, of course, because ferns don't have flowers, but it has fruit similar to the common Icelandic bilberries and, as everyone knows, the Icelandic word for bilberry is *bláber* which some have translated blueberry, which is understandable because blueberries are from the section *Cyanococcus* within the genus *Vaccinium*, which includes bilberries." She stopped to take a breath.

"Slow down," Dooley told her. "So, if I'm hearing you right, you found the fern that blooms and attracts fairies who'll lead us to the treasure?"

"In a manner of speaking…yes." Calix smiled victoriously. "Now I've just got to find them. It's time for a fern hunt." She placed her wide-brimmed sunhat on her head and stood to leave.

"I'm going with you," Cyrano said. "Who knows what you'll find out there, and I don't want you going alone."

"Didn't I tell you he's a wonderful brother?" Calix beamed. "Such a dear!"

"Dooley, do you mind if we take a break from the tin whistle lessons?" Cicely asked. "I just thought of something I need to do. Let's meet up after dinner, and we'll run through your song again, okay?"

"Sure, no problem." Red-faced, Dooley watched Cicely leave.

"Hey, Cyrano," Dooley whispered while Calix busied herself with her gardening apron and tools. "Do you think Cicely thinks I'm…you know…an idiot? I mean, with all my staring and stuff. I try not to, but it's her voice. It makes me all…drooly."

"Don't worry about it, man," Cyrano answered. "You're not the first guy to be hypnotized by her. She probably doesn't even notice."

"Oh, good. That's a relief."

"But I will say this, you just gave yourself a great nickname. See ya, Drooly!"

Cyrano gave Dooley a salute and followed Calix out the front door.

"Pay no attention to that boy with a beak. He thinks he's so cool, but he's really a geek," said Clio as soon as they had left. "I've been waiting to speak to you all afternoon long. But my family's been measuring, pestering and teaching you songs."

"What did you need to talk to me about?"

"I need a job, a chore, a duty, a task. If there's something I can do, you only need to ask."

"A job?"

"Yes, a job for a Rhymer, a person who speaks spells and charms. I'm not the best ever, but at least my spells should do you no harm."

"Actually, I do have something I wanted to ask you about." Dooley flipped through his notebook.

"Several days ago, I walked out to the ash tree in our front field. While I was there, I stepped on a basket with a bunch of berries in it. After I smashed the berries, I wiped the goopy stuff from my sneaker onto the tree. All of a sudden, the berry goo started burning words into the trunk. I've been trying to remember what it said, and I think I've finally got it. Right here: 'It takes a spell to break a spell. A lute, a flute, a toot may rout the root. Before dusk's knell, save us from this beastly cell.'"

Clio read and reread the writing in the notebook. She looked at Dooley and opened her mouth to speak but closed it and read the writing again. Eventually she said, "To break another's spell, one must be a Rhymer of the highest degree. I can barely write my own spells. Why would you choose me?"

"Well, for one thing, you're the only Rhymer I know. But seriously, Clio, I really think you can do this. I saw you make that baseball fly through the air and slam into the wall. You've definitely got skills."

"Levitation is baby stuff, Spell-Speaking 101. Breaking a curse," she whispered, "On the other hand, is not so easily done."

"We know what the curse is: Birna turned all of Olaf's children into animals who are only awake for a couple of weeks every fifty-one years. Can you do something with that? Maybe the tin whistle Cicely is teaching me to play will 'rout the root' and save them. I looked it up, and *rout* means to defeat. I'm not sure what the root is, but maybe it has something to do with the tree. Whatever it is, we do know that only another spell can break Birna's spell." Dooley faced Clio, anxiety written on his features. "You're the only one who can do this."

Clio took the notebook and pencil from Dooley and slid it in front of her. "I'll do my best for our stressed guest with the strange quest."

Dooley sighed. "Thank you, Clio."

She quickly began scratching away at the notebook, formulating possible combinations for her spell.

"I'll leave my notebook with you while I run home to get some stuff for tonight." Dooley looked at the large grandfather clock standing alongside the opposite wall, surrounded by family photos. Only the hands and numbers on the clock's face escaped from being the peachy-pink color of the rest of the room. "It's 4:17. We have less than thirty hours until they all go back to sleep." He shook his head.

Clio looked up from her writing and spoke in confident, deliberate words. "Dooley, valiant hero of old. I grant you strength and a courage so bold. Your victories will be greater than a hundredfold. And your story will be told and retold."

"So...you just said a spell, right? And now all of this will work out?" he asked, hopefully.

"No, Dooley, that was as magical as a greeting card. Believe it or not, writing a real spell is very hard." She rolled her eyes dramatically.

"Oh. Well, thanks anyway."

Chapter 19

FAIRIES IN FLIGHT

Dooley's mother was weeding the flowerbed by the front steps when he arrived home. "Well, hello, stranger," she said as she sat back on her heels and wiped the sweat from her forehead. "I was beginning to think you'd run away from home to join the circus."

"Hey, you're the one who wanted me to make friends."

"I know. I'm kidding. I just miss you."

"Would it be okay if Cyrano and I use Dad's old tent? We were thinking about camping out in the field. Supposed to be a good night for it."

"Since when do you like camping?"

"I've always liked camping...sort of."

Rose slapped a mosquito just as it landed on her arm. "These darn things are eating me alive!"

Dooley pulled out a tiny, flattened bag of yellow cream from his shorts pocket. "Here. Put this on your bites. It works like crazy."

"Well, thanks… What is it?"

"Something Cyrano's sister Calix gave me. So, can I use the tent?"

"I guess so." She looked at the bag uncertainly. "It's in the garage. Just make sure you take care of it. Your dad's had it since he was your age."

Dooley easily found the tent in its faded red bag. He unzipped it, noticing a musty smell as he looked for the accompanying metal tent pegs and ropes. The folded tent was the same reddish-orange as the bag with a gray top. Everything looked in order, so Dooley zipped the bag shut and dragged it to the front yard.

Next, he went inside to find his backpack. "Remember home. Remember home," he muttered to himself as he walked around the house looking for things to bring with him. He picked up a framed picture with the words HOME SWEET HOME stitched on a cream background. His grandmother had made it for Dooley's parents for their first apartment. He slipped it in his bag. Dooley saw his father's third place bowling trophy. He weighed it in his hand for a moment but decided it was too big and set it back on the shelf.

Next, he spotted the smooth, wooden matryoshka figurine his mother had bought when she was a teenager visiting

Europe with her school. As a boy, Dooley had enjoyed opening the little Russian girl to find a smaller version inside. After he had removed all six girls, he would line them up in descending order and examine their delicately painted features. He added her to his backpack, too.

Dooley wasn't sure if he had found enough items or if the things he did find were even what Ambrose had in mind when he made the list, but he decided to move on to the kitchen. He got out bread and peanut butter to make several sandwiches to share with Cyrano. As he looked in the pantry for jelly, he found new ones added to his father's ever-growing collection. One caught his eye in particular—*A Taste of Scandinavia*. He read the first few ingredients on the purple label: "Raspberries, elderberries, strawberries, sour cherries, cloudberries, and crabapples…" He grabbed the unopened jar and slid it into his backpack.

After he had made enough peanut butter sandwiches to feed all the enchanted animals in Peacock Valley, Dooley put the entire stack of them—along with some apples, granola bars, and cheese crackers—in a plastic grocery bag. Then he stuffed the bag into his backpack.

Later, through trial and error and with the help of Cyrano, Dooley pitched the tent under the long branches of the ash tree. Sitting on the uneven ground inside the tent, the boys ate some of the sandwiches while they waited for it to get dark.

"So, Calix said you're supposed to stand outside just after sunset and hold these fern seeds in your hand," Cyrano said as he carefully unwrapped a white handkerchief covered in tiny daisies. A pile of yellow seeds, each the size of a pinhead, were heaped in the center of his cupped palm. "She said the fairies are supposed to swarm around you, and then they'll lead you to treasure."

"Was it hard to find the right fern?"

"It took a while, but Calix is pretty positive that this is the one. When we found it, she started jumping up and down. Then she gave me this long lecture about ferns and cross-pollination. I zoned out after about two minutes."

Dooley looked out the open slit in the front of the tent to check the sky. He saw only the deep blue of a summer evening without any of the vibrant pinks and oranges of the sun's early moments of setting.

"Oh, I almost forgot." Cyrano pulled out a round, plastic container from his duffel bag.

"This is from Celeste. Tomorrow's her birthday, but she begged Mom to go ahead and made her cupcakes tonight."

Dooley took the container and opened it. Inside he found a yellow cupcake with mounds of pink icing and multi-colored, star-shaped sprinkles. Nestled next to the cupcake was a note.

He read it aloud.

"'Dear Dooley, I asked Mom to bake these now since you may die in a fiery battle tomorrow and not be able to come to my party. Love, Celeste. P.S.- I will not know for sure until my birthday, but I think my power is going to be flying. I found feathers in my bed this morning. Clio said I am probably molting (and it is revolting).'"

"Wow. I hope her power isn't prophecy," said Cyrano.

"No kidding. The 'fiery battle' thing doesn't exactly make me feel confident."

During a lull in the conversation, they split the cupcake and washed it down with a bottle of water. Dooley looked out the tent again, his heart fluttering with nervous anticipation. Cyrano found his mother's watch in the front pocket of Dooley's backpack and checked the time. "It's eight o'clock. We've got about an hour until sunset."

"Let's look at the list one more time," Dooley said. He felt his nervousness wane a bit with the prospect of a task to complete instead of just silent, worried waiting. Everything was accounted for, including two pairs of gravity-defying shoes from Crispin, Cashel's animal statues sitting in two plastic pet carriers at the back of the tent and a forest green, cable-knit sweater from Granny Gibbs.

"Leave it to Granny to give you a sweater in the middle of June," Cyrano said, shaking his head.

"She said it'll protect me. Maybe it's like a bullet-proof vest," Dooley said, hopefully.

"She also said magical tree fortresses are usually chilly," countered Cyrano.

"Still…I'm going to wear it."

"She made one for me, too." Cyrano pulled a bundle of navy knitting out of his duffel bag. "I guess it couldn't hurt."

Dooley reorganized the contents of his backpack, placing important items in the front pockets for easy access. Before putting it with the brass compass, the piece of broken mirror, and the tin whistle, he held Ambrose's journal, nearly overcome with a mixture of emotions for this worn, leather-bound book. He thumbed through the pages until he suddenly stopped midway through, his fingers sensing something different about this page. Upon further inspection, he realized two pages were stuck together. He carefully pulled them apart. The lines on the revealed pages were written in a swirl across both sides. It was as if Ambrose had written his words in the trail of a butterfly in flight.

He read the lines to Cyrano: "*Dúfa warned me to be on my guard, for the Valkyrie is a sly one. Birna will coax me into forgetting the world outside—the moon, the stars, the sun. She will cause my eyes to see what I desire, except my desire be escape, for there is none. She will know I am there when she hears me in the dark corridors as I run. She will catch the scent of my fears, my tears, my souvenirs of yesteryears, and then I am done.*"

"Wow," said Cyrano. He looked at his friend intently.

"Yep," Dooley sighed. "At least we know a little more about what we're up against."

"So, we're still going through with it?"

"We're still going through with it. You getting any dangerous smells?"

Cyrano sniffed the air. "Nothing unusual. Just your basic outdoor scents."

"Okay. Then, let's go."

The boys pulled the heavy, hooded sweaters over their t-shirts. Then they found the shoes Crispin had made and slipped them on, leaving their sneakers in the tent. Dooley shouldered his backpack and exited the flap, followed by Cyrano.

Cyrano handed the wrapped bundle of seeds to Dooley.

Just as the last slice of the sun dipped into the horizon, Dooley peeled back the corners of the handkerchief and spilled the seeds into his other hand. Clouds parted to reveal a bright, oblong-shaped moon. The boys held their breath and waited. The cicadas, katydids and crickets were peculiarly silent as if someone had pushed a giant MUTE button.

Suddenly a flock of blinking lights buzzed toward them, aiming at Dooley's outstretched hand like an arrow. One by one, the tiny lights picked up the seeds and darted past his side. Soon his hand was empty, and the lights were zooming in circles around him like thread tightly wound around a spool. It gave the illusion that Dooley was spinning like a top, though he was standing still.

"Dooley!" Cyrano shouted. "Are you alright?"

Dooley's eyes were tightly shut. He heard Cyrano's voice, but he was afraid to speak. He thought if he opened his mouth, something might fly in.

The buzzing sound began to meld into a familiar tune. "Zummm, zummm, zuh-zuh, zummm, zummm, zuh…" Within the droning of the buzzing lights, Dooley heard the notes Cicely had taught him on the recorder. He hummed along with the buzzing melody, softly at first and then louder. All at once the buzzing stopped.

When Dooley found enough courage to cautiously open his right eye, the lights paused in mid-air and slowly— almost as if they were in slow motion—filed away from Dooley in a line. He saw one of the lights as it hovered an inch from his face. "Fireflies," he whispered. The insect held the seed with its front legs, its abdomen pulsing with yellow light.

Once Dooley was released from the swarm, they quickened their pace until they had regained their former frenzied momentum. As they neared the tree, he followed their glowing trail and watched as the fireflies chased their leader, dashing over and under the branches, bursting through leaves with explosive speed.

Eventually the group landed above a patch of moss clinging to the rough bark. With the timing and precision of a marching band, the fireflies positioned themselves on the tree to form a message:

LEAVE A GIFT

As soon as Dooley and Cyrano had read the words out loud, the insects changed positions and another message appeared. It said:

WAIT FOR SUNRISE

Again, the fireflies flitted to form a different message once the boys had finished reading it. The final message instructed:

LIFT THE MOSS

A second later the fireflies had vanished, dispersed into the field and the darkness.

The boys approached the section of the tree where the fireflies had landed. Cyrano retrieved a flashlight from his duffel bag and shined it on the tree. Dooley gently ran his fingers along the raised, vertical strips of gray bark until he came to the patch of thick moss. He tried to pry the edges loose, looking for a hinged door or sliding panel, but all he found was ordinary, furry, green moss.

"Maybe it won't move until we leave a gift and come back to check it at sunrise," Cyrano offered. "Maybe the fireflies told us the messages in the order we should do them."

"Okay. So what gift should we leave?"

"I don't know. What do you feed a magical tree? Something from the Keebler elves?"

Dooley took off his backpack and began to rummage inside. "How about this?" He held up a jar.

"Jelly?"

"Sure. One of the ingredients is the kind of fruit I found in a basket by this tree. Cloudberries, I think. My dad said it's a really unusual kind of fruit."

"Good enough for me." Cyrano took the jar from Dooley and removed the lid with a pop. "It's too bad we didn't bring the peanut butter, too." Cyrano placed the jar at the base of the tree, finding flat ground amongst a jumble of tree roots.

For good measure, Dooley added the wooden matryoshka doll his mother had brought back from her school trip. "And just in case they don't like the jelly..."

Chapter 20

SUMMER
SOLSTICE

When the boys re-entered the tent, they were exhausted and collapsed into their sleeping bags without stopping to remove their shoes or sweaters. Despite his exhaustion, Dooley slept restlessly, plagued by a recurring dream. In the dream, he was cornered by a giant, hissing firefly who—when broken in two at its abdomen—opened to reveal another firefly and another, until he was completely surrounded by a menacing swarm. Each time he reached the moment when the firefly horde was about to strike, he was startled awake, drenched in sweat and tangled inside his sleeping bag.

He reached for the watch to check the time—12:20 a.m. 2:50 a.m. 3:15 a.m. After determining it was too early for sunrise, Dooley would take out the sharp corner piece of the broken mirror and examine it for any movement. He would tilt it, catching the moonlight through the open tent flap but seeing only an empty room in the reflection.

An hour before sunrise Dooley had finally fallen into a deep sleep. If it wasn't for the scratching and snarling coming from the back of the tent, both boys might have overslept the dawn. When they were finally roused from sleep, they investigated the noises coming from the plastic crates.

They saw Cashel's statues, now living, breathing animals. Through the bars of one of the crates, Dooley saw a cat's paw, flexing and extending its claws to scratch the plastic door. Two long tusks poked through the bars of the other pet carrier and a grunting sound came from within.

The boys sat in the dark tent, quickly eating more of the peanut butter sandwiches and all the apples, sharing their crusts and cores with their caged friends. Then they exited the tent, each holding a crate.

When they reached the flat ground at the base of the tree where they had left their gifts, the first rays of the sun began to creep beyond the field. They found only an empty jar—licked clean of any residue—and no matryoshka doll. Dooley put the empty jar in his backpack. They looked at each other, and Cyrano nodded his head toward the tree and the patch of moss just at their eye level.

Dooley set his crate down—generating a series of grunting and scuffling—and ran his hand along the edge of the moss. This time, he easily lifted the patch to reveal a round, wooden knob.

"Here goes," he said as he pressed the knob. The boys heard a sequence of creaking sounds starting at the base of the tree and moving well above their heads. It sounded like an antique, whirring machine.

Without seeing them, Dooley sensed the interior of the tree was full of metal springs and clicking cogs all working together in the dark to unlock a passageway. Moments later, a portion of the tree bark—a 3-foot by 5-foot rectangle—receded and slid open with a groan. The boys peeked into the dark doorway and saw a long set of stairs spiraling down, underground.

They opened the crates and gently pulled out the animals. Cyrano held the creature that looked like Dúfa. It had the snowy white head of a dove and the body of a yellow tabby cat. Though it looked like fur, its back was actually covered with tiny, yellow feathers. The dove/cat purred and cooed as it snuggled into the crook of Cyrano's arm. Dooley held the Egill-like creature. It had the body of a beaver—complete with a giant, flat tail—and the head of a warthog. It fought Dooley, shoving its long tusks into Dooley's chest.

"Wanna trade?" Dooley asked, wrestling the warthog/beaver so that its sharp tusks pointed away from him.

"No, I'm good." Cyrano smiled and stroked the soft feathers of his creature's back.

Eventually, the fight went out of the warthog/beaver, and he settled into Dooley's arms with an air of indignant resignation.

"I guess I finally wore him out," said Dooley. "Looks like I'm just too strong for him."

"Well, he was born this morning, so you just wrestled a baby. You must be really proud."

"Shut up," Dooley said as he examined the scratches on his arms. "Okay, so here's the plan: we bring these guys down to find the underground area where they do the roll call, and we trade them out with the real ones. We convince Dúfa and Egill that we've been sent by their brother Homer ("Humli," corrected Cyrano.) Humli…whatever, to help them escape."

"What makes you think they'll go with us?"

"I've been thinking about that. I'll show them the picture Granny gave us of Ambrose. Maybe they'll recognize him."

"Good idea."

"And we have to do all of this before sunset."

"Right, and without Birna and Olaf finding us."

"Which reminds me…" Dooley removed the swan feather from his backpack. "Take this feather and rub it on you so she won't be able to smell us."

Cyrano took the feather. "What a weird summer this is turning out to be," he said.

"And remember," Dooley continued as he used the feather while balancing his creature, now snoring. "We can't walk on the ground and be ready to pull the bandana over your eyes. Have you got the map?"

"In my pocket," Cyrano answered. "Want me to hold the compass, too?"

"Sure." He handed it to Cyrano.

"Did you check the mirror?"

"Oh yeah, I almost forgot." Dooley reached into his backpack and found the mirror. "The room is still empty. Nobody's there."

Cyrano looked up at the slowly brightening sky. "We'd better go, or they'll do the roll call without us."

"This is it…" Dooley paused, searching for the strength to move forward into the dark, unknown spiraling down before him.

"Faith is to believe what you don't see, and the reward of this faith is to see what you believe," quoted Cyrano.

Dooley gave his friend a long, hard look. He watched as Cyrano's eyeglasses—smudged lenses and thick, black frames—slowly slipped down the steep pitch of his nose. He saw Cyrano stand a little straighter, pulling back his bony shoulder blades like a soldier at attention. Dooley realized Cyrano was trying to convince both of them that they were brave enough for what lie ahead. Still, he knew Cyrano's heart was beating just as fast as his own.

Crack! Dooley heard branches breaking to his right near a clump of scraggly trees, followed by shushing. "Is anybody there?" he asked.

He heard a whistle—*who-oo, who-oo, whooo*—then, the sound of more branches snapping. Soon, the boys saw they were surrounded by Mulligans. Everyone—from Celeste to Granny Gibbs—stepped forward to make a wide circle around the tree.

"We'll be right here," Callidora called, "just a whistle away."

Dooley steadily scanned the encouraging faces staring back at him. When his eyes met Clio's, she told him, "Rehearse the verse to break the curse. My spell is in the notebook's end. If it fails, at least remember it was penned by a friend."

A new face was added to the familiar Mulligan clan.

This one was pale with dark hair and glasses. He wore a lopsided grin.

"That's my dad," Cyrano said, though it was instantly obvious to Dooley who he was. "Looks like everyone's here to see us off." Cyrano pointed to their left. Old Homer stood several feet from the Mulligans, leaning on his cane. He nodded to the boys.

Dooley squared his shoulders and hugged his sleeping warthog/beaver firmly, jostling him slightly and producing a snort. "Okay, let's go."

Chapter 21

ROLL CALL

Remembering they shouldn't touch the ground but seeing this idea as suddenly ludicrous, Dooley lifted his foot to place it on the wall, hesitated, and then returned it to the entrance threshold. His rational understanding of gravity prevented him from moving forward. Cyrano looked at him with raised eyebrows and mouthed the question, "What's wrong?"

Dooley tried to recall Crispin's advice about the shoes. *Take a running leap*, he'd said. *It'll be a lot easier to get up on the wall.* Clinging tightly to his snoring creature, Dooley took a deep breath. Then he leaped onto the packed dirt of the wall, nearly skidding. He felt the shoes cling to the dirt as if they were magnetized to it. Once he stopped fighting the fear he would fall, Dooley realized he felt an invisible board propping him up, keeping his body parallel to the ground. The shoes seemed to infuse his legs and back with a magical rod to help him walk in this unnatural way.

Cyrano jumped onto the wall just after him. The thick folds of the sweater Granny had made for him swaddled themselves around the sleeping dove/cat so that Cyrano could have his hands and arms free. He tapped Dooley to show him, and Dooley realized he could also release his creature.

The boys continued in this manner—walking on the wall, pausing for distant sounds, avoiding glowing torches mounted along the way, and carrying their creatures in knitted papooses—until they came to the end of the stairs.

The bottom of the stairway opened onto a spacious foyer leading to four hallways. The floor was covered in black and white checkered tiles. Mounted on the walls in between the open spaces leading to the halls, Dooley saw torches housed in intricately designed bronze sconces burning above narrow tables. Each table was topped with a large, blue vase full of flowers. The colors of the room were muted by the low, flickering lights.

Cyrano took out the compass and map from his pocket, checking for southeast. He pointed to one of the doorways and they continued walking on the wall. After they entered the hall, Dooley noticed the walls changed from packed dirt to wallpaper and the ceiling was raised. Chandeliers—hung every six feet—held a dozen candles each. Dooley felt exposed and vulnerable by the abundant light.

When he reached for the hood on his sweater to cover his head, Dooley realized the sweater was no longer dark green. Now it matched the floral pattern of the wallpaper. He pulled the sweater down, stretching it past his feet. He was camouflaged almost completely. Cyrano helped him cover his backpack with the sweater. Soon, both boys had blended in with the wall with the exception of their shoes and faces, especially Cyrano's long nose.

Before they could continue walking, they heard whispered voices behind and below them. The boys pressed themselves against the wall, burying their faces in their sweaters.

"Oh, Adar! How can this be the last day of the Roaming?" said a soft, female voice. "I'm loathed to think of sleeping for one and fifty summers before we wakest again." She began to cry.

"Serena, dearest sister," said a male voice, consolingly. "Weepest not. We must hurry to the Counting or we are certain to feel the wrath of our father."

They scurried on, past the boys, claws or talons clipping along the tile floor quickly. Once they were sure the creatures had passed, Dooley and Cyrano stood and resumed walking in the same direction as the creatures.

After several minutes, they reached the end of the hall. They walked through the doorway into another foyer. This time they were confronted with eight closed doors. Cyrano consulted his compass and pointed to one of the doors. As they crept near it, they noticed it was slightly ajar. Dooley pushed it open, causing the ancient hinges to creak. His heart beat wildly as he retreated into the shadows of the ceiling.

Dooley and Cyrano heard fifty hushed voices through

the open door. They knew they had reached the room for the roll call. Dooley took out the mirror from his backpack, careful not to cut himself on the sharp edges. He saw the gold and cream patterned wallpaper and the crimson couch, the same room he saw every time he looked into the mirror. Only this time the room was filled with animals. A falcon-headed bear, a lizard with the tail of a spider monkey, a squat kangaroo with the face of a raccoon, and no Olaf.

Dooley cracked the door open a few more inches, just enough to allow them to enter. They stepped onto the ceiling and the animals let out a collective gasp. Dooley quickly withdrew the photographs of Ambrose and his wife Rebecca from his backpack. He scanned the group, looking for Dúfa. When he saw her, Dooley walked down the wall toward her and held the framed photographs out for Dúfa to see. The glow from the kerosene lamp on the end table flickered across the picture as she blinked her bird eyes several times.

Keer, she hissed to her brothers and sisters in a language neither Dooley nor Cyrano had ever heard before, *Freegla selfra!*

The creatures continued to murmur as before but with a look of fear in their wide eyes. Egill joined his sister at the edge of the room. Dooley was surprised how quickly he was able to move despite the imbalance caused by his wooden leg. Egill still carried the leather satchel across his chest.

Dooley uncovered the bundle swaddled inside his sweater so that Egill and Dúfa could see it. The warthog/beaver opened its eyes groggily and shook its tusk. Egill harrumphed and narrowed his eyes skeptically. Cyrano approached them and showed them his creature, also just waking up.

The dove/cat stepped lightly down from his arms and began to explore the room and the other creatures. Dúfa jumped into the space it vacated and Cyrano wrapped her up, covering her until only her beak showed above the folds of his sweater.

It took a little coaxing to get the warthog/beaver to leave the warmth of Dooley's sweater. When Dooley had finally shoved it away and it had landed on the carpeted floor, it lunged toward Egill. Always looking for a fight, Egill prepared to engage but Dooley scooped him up before their tusks could collide.

With their new passengers in tow, they retreated to the ceiling to make their exit. Just as they reached the lintel above the doorway, the door was thrown open and a mountain of a man entered. He was followed close behind by one of his children, a creature with the sleek, red body of a fox and the bumpy, green-gray head of a toad.

"Mine children!" Olaf bellowed.

Dooley and Cyrano pressed against the wall, covering themselves with their camouflaging sweaters.

The creatures assembled below bowed in submission to their father. Forty-eight backs—some scaly, some furry, some feathered—were all that could be seen of the creatures, with the exception of two. Being newly born that morning, these two didn't know Olaf's rules about bowing and scraping before their father.

The Dúfa imposter sat in a corner licking a front paw with her tiny bird tongue, and the Egill imposter sawed its tusks against the leg of the couch. Fortunately for the phony creatures, Olaf missed this irregularity in the usual morning roll call. Instead, he used his sleeve to shine the gold medallion that hung from a chain around his neck. By the time his medallion had an acceptable shine and he fully looked at his children, they were no longer bowing. A few of the creatures stepped in front of the imposters to screen them from Olaf's vision.

"Mine children!" he repeated. "Once again, we gather here on this, the last morn of a Glorious Roaming! It is the will of thine benevolent and magnificent stepmother to allow this. Her affection for us wast so great that she didst charm our souls so we might live on for many centuries to come. We age but a year for every one and fifty years we sleep. In this way, I am a mere dozen years older than I was when Lady Birna and I first wed."

"Seventeen," a voice piped up from the crowd. Shocked, the other creatures inhaled in unison.

"Who dost intrude upon mine speech?" Olaf thundered.

The crowd of creatures parted and a brown hound dog with the wooly head of a sheep stepped forward, trembling, and bowed low. "It is I, Vígi, thy third born son."

"Rise, Vígi, third born son of Olaf," he growled. "Thou art bold to speak so freely. What was it thou deemed so imperative thou must disdain thy father in this manner?"

"Lord, I said only that we have seen *seventeen* Roamings not a dozen, so thou art *seventeen* years older since that first day though nigh unto nine hundred years have passed. And may I say, lord, thy youthful manliness…"

"Quiet, dog!" Olaf roared. "I see thou hast used these years to improve thy arithmetic skills. Now step forward and take thy lashes for thy impudence. I will provide something for thy superior counting skills…"

Olaf reached under his velvet cloak and pulled out a braided, leather whip. He gave Vígi five lashes across his back. For every strike, Dooley heard the whistling of the whip through the air and the groan of the cowering creature. He also felt Egill's response, a tightening of muscles and an intake of breath. Egill's body was empathetic to his brother's pain.

"Depart from mine chambers, ye ungrateful and shameful children! I wilt see ye all upon the setting of the sun." As he dismissed them, Olaf stood just inside the door.

Dooley risked showing his face to watch as Olaf retrieved a rolled paper from inside his cloak. He untied the string and held it between his powerful hands. Dooley saw that the paper was a map similar to the one Ambrose had drawn in his journal.

As each creature passed Olaf, his medallion would glow, and a dot would appear on the map. As the creatures left the room, the dots quickly spread away from the center of the tree, down the twisting corridors, and eventually out into the field.

The creatures herded the imposter animals out the door with little resistance. The medallion awarded them a dot on the map as well.

That must be how Olaf keeps track of his kids during the Roaming, Dooley thought.

Vígi was the last to leave. His back was cut and swollen. Blood red stripes covered the ridge between his shoulder blades. He crept forward with his tail tucked between his cowering hind legs.

"Seventeen," Olaf snarled as he kicked Vígi out the door, whimpering. Olaf turned to look at himself in the large mirror hanging just across from the couch.

As he paused to admire his reflection and stroke his red-orange moustache, he frowned, noticing a sprinkling of unwanted gray mixed in with the red. While Olaf was occupied plucking out the gray hairs, Dooley and Cyrano tiptoed to the doorframe and stepped over the lintel to re-enter the hallway.

Chapter 22

ROUT THE ROOT

As soon as they had left Olaf's room, Dooley realized he didn't have a Phase Two in his plan. Trying to push down the feeling of panic rising inside of him, he walked along the ceiling silently scolding himself for assuming they wouldn't make it this far.

After they had walked a few yards, Cyrano tapped Dooley's shoulder. They stopped, and Cyrano handed him the compass. The red-tipped needle pointed north behind them and to the left. *How could that be?* Dooley wondered to himself. Southeast should be behind them now that they were walking away from Olaf's room.

Egill wriggled his head out of the sweater and tapped one tusk on the space between the S and the E on the compass. He nodded his head as if to say they should continue to follow that bearing. Dooley shrugged and walked on.

They wound up and down noiseless, nearly identical corridors for half an hour. Just when Dooley was beginning to think they were walking in circles, they came to a long, narrow hallway with a dead end. He checked the compass. Southeast was straight ahead. They walked a little farther down the hallway noticing that the wallpaper in this section had gradually changed. Instead of a simple floral pattern, the design had morphed into a field thick with flowers and partially hidden animals.

Cyrano pulled out the folded map and saw several tunnels ending with X's. One had a drawing of a framed painting just above the X. He showed the map to Dooley. When they looked at the end of the hall, it narrowed until it stopped at a wall covered almost entirely with a large portrait of a woman. She wore a floor-length, shimmering gown in the same color as her hair—silver. She held a golden shield in one hand and a sword in the other.

They inched down the wall a little closer, then stopped when Dúfa gasped. All of them watched as the eyes of the woman in the portrait moved, as if searching for something in the dark hallway. Dooley and Cyrano froze. Dooley knew it was Birna's magic. This portrait was guarding something behind the wall. But how could he get past it without raising an alarm?

In his mind, he went through the items in his backpack: Broken mirror, pocketknife, empty jelly jar, fountain pen and journal, feather, chain links, wristwatch, and Cicely's recorder. Should he play the tune Cicely had taught him? What if he slashed the painting with the pocketknife? He couldn't know for sure what would grant him access to this secret room, but he knew if he made the wrong choice, it was certain they'd be found out.

As Dooley stood pondering his options, he heard footsteps coming toward them. He and Cyrano flattened themselves against the ceiling, hiding from those who passed below them.

"I wilt see about these gray hairs, Padda, mine son." It was Olaf, speaking to one of his children.

"Aye, father," answered a croaking voice. "Thou art too young to suffer so."

"Indeed. Lady Birna's glowing orb will return to me mine vim and vigor."

"Is it a powerful device?"

"Why, yes! I have used it once before a few Roamings past, and it cured mine rheumatism."

"And mine esteemed stepmother does not object?"

"Object? Certainly not! She is mine wife, is she not? And am I not the lord of this kingdom?"

"Yes, father!"

"Furthermore, she has flown away, and wilt not return until eventide. But I learnt how to enter this chamber when I wast here last."

Dooley peeked past his sweater to watch Olaf and Padda—the same creature with the head of a toad and the body of a fox Dooley had seen with Olaf at the Roll Call—as they approached the painting. Olaf lifted the medallion he wore around his neck.

"I wilt say an incantation and the wall wilt open for

me. You, Padda my son, wilt tarry and wait for me here."

"Yes, father, it be mine pleasure to obey."

"There is none other of mine children I would entrust with such a task. You must stand guard as I must leave the passage open, but you shan't let anyone enter. As long as you stand by the open door, 'twill not close."

"Yes, father. I understand."

Olaf stood just a few feet from the painting and the woman's eyes, swiveled to face him. He held his medallion in front of her and cleared his throat.

"*Fitlay, Breegla, Heert! Leeday, Jorgna, Kreet!*"

As soon as he had uttered the last syllable of the spell, both the medallion and the eyes of the woman in the painting glowed. The wall, along with the painting, slid aside to reveal a small room.

After he had watched his father step inside, Padda turned to face anyone who might approach him. Dooley couldn't imagine how this squat, toad-faced creature could be very threatening as a guard dog, but he wasn't willing to risk having Padda see him.

Dooley crept as slowly and quietly as he could to the open room. Twenty feet away, all he could see was a faint, blue glow spilling out into the hall. By the time he reached the opening, Olaf had reappeared.

"Ahhh! Much better!" he bellowed, stretching his massive arms in the air. "Look, Padda! Tell me. Dost thou see any gray in mine beard?"

"No, father! 'Tis redder than the sun at its setting! And thy face, it has no lines or creases! Tis a wonder, indeed!"

"I feel like a man of twenty!"

"But what is this magic?" asked Padda.

"Lady Birna told me it is the whole source of her mighty powers. She keeps it here so that I can watch over it for her."

"How dost it work?"

"It is a bright, blazing orb of light and heat. Tis connected to the root of this enchanted tree. They cannot live without each other—the orb and the tree. If one fails then both fail."

"Tis a wonder," Padda repeated.

"Come now. I must rest from this errand."

Olaf began to walk back down the long corridor, but Padda stopped him. "Father, shouldst we leave the room open?"

"Oh…of course not! Do you think me simple-minded?" Olaf answered. "I wilt close the room with the same incantation but in reverse."

He held the medallion up to the opening and said, "*Kreet, Jorgna, Leeday! Heert, Breegla, Fitlay!*"

The wall and the painting re-emerged slowly with the sound of stone scraping against stone. Soon the wall was fully replaced, and everything was returned to its original position.

"Those words of Lady Birna send shivers along mine spine," said Padda as his long, furry tail twitched briskly. "What dost it mean, Father?"

"I know not. I only know that it works."

"I have heard some of mine brothers and sisters speak in such a way. Perhaps they can translate the phrases."

"Is that so?" Olaf asked as they walked away from the portrait.

"Yes, thy first born daughter Dúfa is one. Methinks she

has many secrets hidden inside her tiny, bird brain."

Dúfa's head jerked out of Cyrano's sweater. She narrowed her eyes at the pair as they reached the end of the hallway and turned left.

Almost out of earshot, they heard Olaf say, "Padda, thou art a sly fox indeed."

Chapter 23

BE BRAVE

Dooley considered following Olaf and Padda but decided against it. He knew they needed to get the medallion Olaf wore if they were to get inside the secret room, but they needed a plan first. And in order to make a plan, they needed to find a place where they could sit and talk without fear of discovery.

Dooley pulled the compass out of his pocket and checked his bearings again. Though only moments ago, it had indicated southeast to be in the direction of the portrait, now that Dooley had his back to the secret room, the letters of the compass had shifted. Now when the red tip of the needle quivered at the N, southeast was the opposite from the wall with the portrait.

Dooley began his quiet, tentative trudging back to the

end of the corridor. When the hallway opened to four alternate routes, Dooley looked to see which way the compass advised them to take, knowing that he could no longer guarantee that the needle would point to north. This time the needle spun violently in the case, past the N, E, S, and W, and then around again.

Deciding he required more light to see the compass, Dooley climbed down from the dark ceiling and stood on the wall. When it finally stopped spinning, the red tip pointed up—not north but actually through the glass of the case to the ceiling. The needle had come unhinged from the axis, and it was quivering nervously.

Dooley looked above him at the highest elevation of the ceiling. He walked back up the wall and examined the dimly lit corner where the wall and ceiling met. He felt along the wooden beams that ran the length of the area just at the end of the hallway until he found gaps in the wood. Four chunks were cut out of the beam, evenly spaced apart so that his fingers fit in each one. With his fingers in place, Dooley pulled down on the beam and something clicked above his head. A door, similar to the attic door leading to Cyrano's room, opened.

Dooley opened the small door the rest of the way and pulled himself through. Cyrano followed, and the trap door swung shut behind them. They were in total darkness. Luckily, Cyrano still had his flashlight in his pocket. As he fumbled with the switch, Dooley tried to comprehend where they were. The smell of sawdust and hay filled his nose.

With his arms extended in front him, Dooley eventually

bumped into something that felt like the woven placemats his mom always kept out on the kitchen table. When Cyrano shined his flashlight in Dooley's direction, they realized they were standing next to a wall of woven straw. Upon further inspection, they saw it was a giant basket like the ones attached to hot air balloons. Two ropes hung in the center.

They climbed inside and saw a hook near their feet where the rope looped through, attaching the rope to the basket. Cyrano examined the ropes with his light and followed their trail several yards up. Dooley shook the ropes, and a pulley dangled and clanked above them. He pulled one side of the rope, and the basket lifted off the ground. Realizing they were in a type of elevator, both boys pulled together, hoisting the basket even higher. The basket slowly lifted, making its way up through a shaft which had been hollowed just wide enough for the basket.

They continued pulling the rope until Dooley could reach out and touch the pulley where it hung from an arm extended from the wall. Dooley was grateful he couldn't see how high they were off the ground. Everything below them was inky black darkness.

Unsure if they were nearing a light or if his eyes had just become accustomed to the darkness, Dooley began to see his surroundings more clearly. Soon he saw a ledge to their left. Throwing their weight simultaneously, the arm pivoted, causing the basket to swing safely to the ledge. They stepped out of the basket and walked through a cave-like hole.

The five-by-five foot room they entered looked like the inside of a beehive. The walls were made of yellow, straw thatch. Branches curved every six inches along the walls, securing the straw. Dooley thought the room was pure sunshine after winding up and down so many dark halls.

"Oh! To be free of this maddening fleece!" shouted Egill, as he attempted to squirm out of Dooley's sweater.

Dooley and Cyrano shushed him at the same time.

"Fear not, boys," Dúfa cooed. "We shan't be found here. This room wast made by Egill and others of our kin. We are safe to speak now."

Dúfa and Egill walked along the straw carpet, happily stretching and scratching. Egill wriggled out of his leather satchel and rolled onto his back.

"Where are we?" Dooley asked, half surprised by the sound of his own voice.

"'Tis ten yards from the ground on the east side of the tree, boy," Egill grunted.

"How come I've never seen this tree house before?" asked Cyrano. "I mean, you'd think I'd notice something this big."

"Mine brother Egill hast a genius for building. He made this room just at the point where the leaves could hide it." Dúfa purred and rubbed against Cyrano's leg affectionately. "To any passers-by, this room looks like the knob left after a limb has been cut from the tree. Tis all bark and leaves from the outside."

"I guess it doesn't hurt to build it in a magic tree either," added Dooley.

"Most of the halls and rooms of Lady Birna's fortress are outfitted with devices for spying on us, her lowly step-children," Egill explained. "Besides this apartment here, there is only the entrance at the base of the tree where one may speak freely."

Dooley and Cyrano plopped down on the floor, exhausted. Dooley opened his backpack and took out the last of their food. They shared their sandwiches, granola bars, and cheese crackers along with the last bottle of water with Dúfa and Egill. Though they were finally allowed to speak, they ate in silence. Dooley couldn't find the words to describe what they had done and seen.

When they had eaten everything, Dooley sat alone in a corner and pulled out Ambrose's journal. A folded paper fell out, onto his lap. It was a note from Clio.

Pure heart and selfless spirit.
Eyes to see and ears to hear it.
Will of iron and mind to steer it.
Though afraid, do not fear it.
Conquer evil and good will cheer it
Creatures trapped in hybrid shells.
Birna's curse—a wicked spell
Can be broken when based on deceit.
Her words will be her own defeat
She promised to be mother to them all.
But a mother's love is not so small
A mother's love can travel time.
It knows no bounds; it draws no lines
Birna made them wretched; she showed no care.
So challenge her claim and end their nightmare
Break the spell with love so pure.

Devotion that will always endure
Learn these words and keep them close;
They may be the key to defeat your foes:

BE BRAVE

SHOCKWAVE

MUST SAVE THE ENSLAVED

LOVE'S LIGHT MAKES RIGHT

THE GOOD FIGHT NEEDS SIGHT

Dooley read over her words several times. Then, he closed his eyes and tried to whisper the spell from memory.

"Cease your mumbling, boy," Egill barked. "'Tis time to devise a scheme."

Dooley closed the notebook and they all scooted closer, making a circle.

"The way I see it, the first thing we need to do is take Olaf's necklace," Cyrano said.

"Right, then we need to use it to open the door to the secret room, so we can destroy that 'orb' thing since it's source of Birna's power," added Dooley.

"Can thou remember the magical incantation to open the door?" Egill asked.

"No," Dooley answered. "It all sounded like gibberish to me."

"I wilt help you, dear boy," Dúfa reassured. "'Tis easy enough. Now, by the close of the Roaming, our father spends most of his time dozing in his chamber. We shouldst start there, methinks."

"And what an idle man is he?" Egill snapped. "For one and fifty years we do naught but sleep and yet he chooses to spend this precious fortnight of freedom in his bed!"

"Assuming we get the necklace from him, how will we ever find the room again?" Cyrano asked. "I was so mixed up by the time we found the portrait…"

"We'll just use the compass, right?" Dooley looked at Dúfa and Egill for confirmation. He took the brass instrument from his pocket.

"But it's the strangest compass I've ever seen. Why doesn't the needle point to north? And how is it that we can keep walking in the direction of southeast? It just doesn't make any sense," said Cyrano.

Egill explained: "S.E. is not southeast. These letters stand for *skapraun eptri*, which means 'annoying backside.' 'Tis Birna's pet name for our dolt of a father. She made this for Olaf many years ago for he wast forever losing his way in the corridors. 'Tis a bewitched instrument which was stolen from that vain and idle man."

"Stolen?" Dooley asked in surprise. "I thought it was just a regular compass. We found it in Ambrose's things."

Egill gave Dúfa a withering look. "'Tis your doing, sister."

"I told Ambrose of the compass when he was a boy. He must've taken it whilst we were sleeping."

"So, whoever is holding it just has to think of where they want to go, and the compass will point in that direction?" asked Cyrano, as he watched the N, E, S, W letters spin around the edge of the dial.

"Yes," answered Dúfa. "If thou but think of finding Olaf's chambers, thou wilt find him."

Reluctant to leave but not wanting to waste too much time lounging in the enchanted tree house, Dooley and Cyrano and their creature companions found their way back down to the winding corridors. As promised, the compass guided them to Olaf's bedroom.

When Dooley reached into his backpack to retrieve the mirror and check Olaf's location, he heard Egill's snores from within his sweater. Dooley looked at Cyrano and saw Dúfa resting her bird head on her front paws, also asleep. He found the watch they had borrowed from Cyrano's mother; it was 4:30 pm. They had less than five hours until sunset and Birna's return. He glanced at Cyrano who he knew had been thinking the same thing: *Would they run out of time?*

Chapter 24

REMEMBER HOME

The mirror showed Olaf stretched out on his crimson couch and toad-faced Padda curled up on the floor beneath him. Both of them seemed to be sleeping. It was now or never. As silently as possible, Dooley opened the door, and both boys stepped over the doorway and into the room. They climbed down the wall, edging toward Olaf as he snoozed on his side, his cheek resting against his clasped hands.

Dooley sighed with relief when he saw the chain and medallion were hanging on the arm of the couch. Carefully, he lifted the chain—nearly dropping it at first because he had underestimated its weight. He slid it into the back pocket of his shorts and climbed back up the wall where Cyrano was waiting for him on the ceiling.

Dooley was already out the door when he heard Dúfa's stifled shriek behind him. When he turned to look at them,

Cyrano was trying to hide himself with the hood of his sweater with one hand and cover Dúfa's beak with the other.

"What? Who art there?" Olaf roared, rubbing the drool from his cheek.

Padda jumped up. His toad eyes darted back and forth, looking for a possible intruder.

"Humli! No!" Dúfa screamed. Her eyes were still closed as she struggled to free herself from the tormenting memories of a dream.

"Shhh!" said Cyrano.

"I know thou art here!" Olaf shouted, now on his feet. "Show thyself, vile trespassers!"

"Run," hissed Egill as he attempted to squirm out of Dooley's sweater. "Now!"

While Dooley was frozen with fear, Egill leapt to the floor and shuffled back into the room. Instantly, he charged Padda. Using his long tusks, he scooped Padda off the ground and threw him in the air.

Dúfa woke up and looked down at her brothers as they tried to bite and stab each other. Cyrano was also watching the skirmish and didn't notice Olaf clambering onto the couch to grab them.

"A-ha!" Olaf cried, victoriously. He roughly pulled Cyrano and Dúfa onto the couch. Then he grabbed Egill by one of his tusks and flung him down next to them. "I see mine own ungrateful children, but who…art thou?" Olaf stuck a pudgy finger in Cyrano's face.

"My name is Cyrano, Cyrano M-M-Mulligan, sir," Cyrano stammered.

"Well, Cyrano Mulligan. Thou art now a captive of Olaf the Peacock, the most heroic of all Viking lords." Olaf reached his hand out to the kerosene lamp on the marble-topped side table. When he pulled it down, a hole opened just below their feet and the couch tipped down toward it, dumping Cyrano, Egill, and Dúfa into darkness. Just as quickly, the floor slid back to cover the hole again.

Olaf clapped his hands together proudly. "Lady Birna will reward me for mine success, I would wager. I didst easily quell a possible overthrow of mine power."

"Father," said Padda, his big eyes resting on the empty arm of the couch.

"Yes, son?" he answered, still beaming.

"Where didst thou lay thine medallion?"

"'Twas here a moment ago…" Olaf began looking under furniture and lifting cushions.

"Dost thou think…is it possible the medallion might have gone down…"

"To the dungeon?" Olaf said, finishing Padda's sentence.

"'Tis the only explanation, mine father."

Pulling the lamp down again, they both peered into the darkness.

"We must find the other way, Padda. Fetch the map."

After they had hustled out of the room, Dooley realized he needed to move quickly. Retrieving the compass with a shaky hand, he found SE and started out alone to find the source of Birna's power.

~

Cyrano, Egill, and Dúfa slid down a long, smooth,

spiraling slide until they reached the bottom and landed in a heap on a dirt floor. Assaulted by utter darkness. Cyrano reached in his pocket for his flashlight, but found only broken pieces.

"'Tis the dungeon," Egill snorted, "a dark and dismal place. Its remoteness is our consolation for it affords us the freedom to speak aloud without fear."

"Are you two okay?" asked Cyrano.

"A mite bruised but whole," answered Dúfa. "I cannot see mine paw in front of mine face," said Dúfa. "How wilt we ever escape?"

Cyrano began to sniff the air.

"What is it, boy?" Egill asked.

"I don't know, but there's a familiar smell coming from over there." Cyrano bent down, blindly feeling for Dúfa and Egill. "Can I carry you?"

Dúfa, followed by Egill, jumped into his sweater pouch, and Cyrano stood carefully.

After taking slow, deliberate steps and frequently pausing to sniff the air, Cyrano eventually turned a corner and saw a glimmer of light ahead. The familiar scent of lavender and lemongrass was increasing.

The light from mounted torches greeted them as they turned another corner. A small hut, similar to Old Homer's cabin, stood against a dirt wall painted a bright blue. A round, yellow sun was painted to the left of the hut, and a moon and stars were painted on the right. Cyrano rubbed his eyes as he looked at a tidy garden growing under the rays of the artificial sun.

A cast iron pot hung over a smoldering fire. Bubbling inside was the source of the scent that had attracted Cyrano. He recognized it now as the smell of his granny's soap. The memory of her suddenly made him aware of his unfortunate predicament.

"Hello?" squeaked a voice.

Cyrano turned to see a slender man in his late twenties. He had pale blond hair and lashes and gentle, light-blue eyes. He wore a white shirt that was rolled up to his elbows and dark suspenders. His gray trousers were fraying at the cuffs and he was barefoot.

"Hello," Cyrano replied. "Where are we?"

"This is my yard, and that is my house," he said, pointing. The man seemed to labor with the effort of finding words. Cyrano wondered when was the last time he had spoken aloud in this lonely place.

"I was an artist—of a sort—many years ago. My paints have been such a comfort to me. I suppose you could call it my gift."

"Oh," Cyrano said. He paused before continuing, "Who are you?"

Just then, Dúfa peeked out of Cyrano's sweater. "Ambrose? Thou art alive?"

She jumped down and ran to the man, purring and rubbing against his worn trousers.

"Dúfa, my friend!" he said as he picked her up and cradled her in his arms.

He suddenly began to cry. Then he plopped down on the dirt floor and sobbed wildly into Dúfa's feathers.

"Wait a minute!" shouted Cyrano. "You're Ambrose? Ambrose Eustace Sullivan?"

The man nodded his head, unable to speak.

"Then…you're my great grandfather!"

Ambrose wailed and wept harder while Egill and Cyrano stared in disbelief.

The four of them remained this way until Egill jumped down from Cyrano's arms and said, "'Tis a touching reunion to be sure, but let us not be overcome. Ambrose, control yourself, man. Thou art playing the fool."

Ambrose wiped his nose on his sleeve and looked at Cyrano.

"What is your name, son?"

"Cyrano."

"Your grandmother is…"

"Dorothea…"

"Oh, my little Dorothea…" Ambrose tasted the name on his lips, trying to summon it from his sluggish mind. "Is she…"

"Alive? Yes, she's very much alive." Cyrano sat down beside Ambrose. "She turned eighty-eight on her last birthday."

"I can't remember what she looked like. I can't remember anything much…anymore." Ambrose looked around at his painted replica of the sky and trees.

Cyrano thought about Ambrose's list. He thought about #10-*Remember Home*.

"Granny still makes the same soap—just like you." Cyrano pointed to the bubbling pot. "With lavender and lemongrass and a pinch of sage. We live right above here, in

Peacock Valley. My mom, Callidora, is your granddaughter. She has hair and eyes just the same colors as yours. I have six brothers and sisters, and we all have powers. Even my neighbor Dooley has a power. He's a Visus, just like you."

"A Visus…" Ambrose pulled his eyebrows down in an effort to concentrate.

"Yes, you can see things, things others can't see. And," Cyrano gestured toward the blue sky of the walls, "you've also gotta be a Voúrtsa—a Brush. I can see the magic in your painting."

Ambrose took slow, labored breaths as he tried to comprehend everything Cyrano was saying. Not wanting to meet Cyrano's direct gaze, he looked down and stroked Dúfa's feathers.

"Granny gave us your journal, and we've come to rescue Olaf's children from the curse." Cyrano grabbed Ambrose's shirt and shook him. "You've got to remember. You've got to remember home and your wife Rebecca and your parents and your brothers. Remember the fields around your house and your cow…um, what was her name…"

"Elsie," Ambrose answered. "My cow was named Elsie. She had…brown spots and a black circle around her eye. I remember her…"

"That's right! What else do you remember?"

"I remember Rebecca making hot coffee for breakfast and muffins. I remember reading to Dorothea. Books about… about…oh, I can't remember anything else." He dropped his head.

"'Tis much for one day, dear Ambrose," purred Dúfa.

"No, 'tis not enough," Egill barked. "Olaf is no doubt in search of his medallion, and Dooley shalt soon be caught. Then what wilt happen to us? We shalt be prisoners alongside this simpleton for all eternity!"

"Oh, I wish we had the rest of the items from your list," said Cyrano.

"My list?"

"Yes, from your journal. We had everything: the swan feather, the tin whistle and the two links of chain. Now it's all in Dooley's backpack. Hopefully, it will at least help him."

"Two links?"

"Yes, you wrote 'two links are better than one' in your journal. Granny gave us a bag of your stuff and pieces of an old, black chain were in it."

"I didn't write it about the chain, Cyrano." Ambrose stood up, dumping Dúfa onto the ground. His expression gradually changed from despair to hope. Ambrose pressed two fingers against his lip as he tried to remember. Cyrano could've sworn the painted sun was shining like a sunrise and glowing right on his great grandfather as he stood.

"I wrote it about life. I felt like I was going it alone. I needed someone to walk with me on this adventure I had planned, but Rebecca wouldn't hear of it. It wasn't just about the thrill of exploration, you see, we needed money. But my Rebecca was always cautious. She was happy to knit and sew and care for Dorothea, but I wanted more. I wish I had listened to her." Ambrose looked around at the earthen walls of his dungeon. "I should've waited for her to be ready. She knitted a carpet for me, a flying carpet, so

I could explore but she didn't want anything to do with this tree."

"Granny never mentioned anything about a flying carpet."

"She wouldn't. It's one of the few things I thought to bring with me here."

Ambrose disappeared into his hut. After a few minutes, he brought out a stiff, tightly woven rug about the size of a loveseat. It was decorated with a zigzag pattern in bold colors. He handed it to Cyrano.

"How does it work?"

"You sit on the rug and command it to rise. Then, you pull the corners to steer."

"Why haven't you used this to fly up the slide? You could've escaped a long time ago!" cried Cyrano.

"I've tried but there's no way to open the trap door at the top. I've flown all through these dark tunnels, but they twist and turn and confound me every time. If only I had my compass…"

"Dooley has it now." They all sat down, dejected again.

"Hush," said Egill, "I hear voices coming."

"This way, Padda…" a deep voice echoed down one of the tunnels.

"It's Olaf," Cyrano whispered.

"In my house, quickly." Ambrose ushered them inside and went to his stool by the fire to stir his pot.

Moments later, Olaf and Padda entered Ambrose's "yard" carrying a torch and a map.

"Deceitful mongrel of a man," Olaf shouted when he reached Ambrose.

"Well, good day to you, too," Ambrose answered as calmly as he could.

"Hush," snapped Padda, "Speak humbly before mine father, troublemaker!"

"Beg pardon, Lord Olaf." Ambrose bowed, mockingly. "I wouldn't want you to sic your attack toad on me. He might give me warts."

"Enough!" Olaf bellowed, his booming voice bouncing through the cavernous tunnels. "I am searching for an item, and thou wilt help me to find it."

"What is it you're looking for?"

"'Tis a simple chain and pendant," Olaf said with feigned detachment. "A trifle really. Not worth much in gold but a sentimental piece."

"I've not seen any kind of jewelry that fits that description, Your Grace. Perhaps we should ask Lady Birna…"

"No!" shouted Olaf before containing his distress. "Uh… no, Lady Birna shouldst not be troubled over such a frivolous matter."

"Thou wilt be our guide through these tunnels and show us where the slide ends," added Padda. "That is the most logical place to look for the medallion."

"What if I'd rather not go with you? I wouldn't want my soap to boil over."

"Thou wilt do as thou are told, lowly swine!" Olaf roared, pointing at Ambrose with a rolled scroll.

Through the partially opened front door, Cyrano listened to the conversation in the yard with growing alarm. Looking down, he saw he was sitting on Ambrose's carpet.

Quietly, he placed Egill and Dúfa in his lap. After taking a deep breath and grasping two corners of the carpet, he yelled, "Rise!" and the carpet hovered a few feet above the ground. "Forward!"

They zoomed out the door with a bang and flew to the place where the three were standing. Without hesitation, Ambrose grabbed the scroll from Olaf and simultaneously tipped over the bubbling pot. Olaf's legs and feet and most of Padda's body were drenched in the hot, waxy liquid. Before they could react, Ambrose had jumped onto the rug as it dashed past them.

The sound of Olaf and Padda screaming faded as they flew down a dark hall. Ambrose snatched a torch from the wall and unrolled the scroll in his lap. He scanned the map for an *AES* in the halls of the dungeon. Once he found it, he said, "Keep down this tunnel until the next fork, then turn left."

When they turned, the *AES* on the map turned left, too. "This is exhilarating!" he yelled in Cyrano's ear to be heard above the whooshing. "I haven't felt this alive in eighty years!"

Chapter 25

FLAMES

It wasn't until they had finally flown up to the last set stairs, that Ambrose and Cyrano realized the door leading to their escape was closed. They looked to their creature companions for help, but the rocking of the carpet ride had caused Egill and Dufa to doze again, and they couldn't be roused.

"Stop!" commanded Cyrano, and the carpet paused inches away from the wooden door. He scanned the mechanism designed to open the door, tracing the path of the chains, sprockets, springs and wheels for a button or a lever to initiate the opening process. "Look, there!" He pointed to a wooden pole extending from the floor several feet from the door. Cyrano was about to dismount from the carpet, when Ambrose stopped him.

"You can't touch the floor!" Ambrose warned. "Birna will know you're here, and it may mean exposure and certain death for your friend!"

"I know. I've got these special shoes my brother made for me that let me walk on the wall. I'll walk over and pull the lever so you can fly out."

"Give *me* the shoes and *I'll* open the door," said Ambrose. "Just after you leave the carpet, command it to return to me."

"But what if the door closes, and you aren't be able to escape?"

Ambrose laid a hand on Cyrano's shoulder. "I'll be fine. I must find your friend."

After he had slipped on Cyrano's shoes, Ambrose stepped onto the wall. As hoped, the lever opened the door, and the carpet flew its occupants out into the early evening light. Just before the door slammed shut, Cyrano jumped off, landing on the ground, and shouted, "Return to Ambrose!" The carpet obeyed. It slid through the narrowing crack and into Ambrose's waiting hands.

"Mom! Dad! Granny!" Cyrano yelled. "Where is everybody?"

"We're here, son," called his father, Lloyd. His family surrounded him as he described their experiences since they had entered the tree.

"After all these years...my Daddy is alive?" Granny Gibbs asked. Cashel had to help her sit down. She crumpled onto a nearby stump, visibly shaken by the news.

"Yes. He's gone back to get Dooley, but he's got to hurry." Cyrano sniffed the air. "I can already smell it."

"What is it, son?" Lloyd asked.

"It smells like a bonfire...a big one. It's the tree."

Calix gasped.

Celeste buried her face in her hands, and Clio hugged her closely.

"We've got to get in and help," said Crispin. He looked down at Cyrano's bare feet. "Where are the shoes I made you?"

"Ambrose has them."

"Well, let's at least go in. We've got to do something," Cashel said, anxiously. "What about the creatures…the ones I made for you? Were you able to trade them out for the real ones?"

"Yes."

"Well, maybe they know how to open the door. Where are they?"

"Good idea. Egill, Dúfa," Cyrano called. He looked around, but they were nowhere to be seen. "They were just here. I promise."

"They may still be here, methinks," said Homer, leaning on his cane. "We have not the power to see them, but I feel…they are near."

Purring softly, Dúfa rubbed against Homer's leg, unseen but still felt by the old man.

"But I saw them…really, I did."

"No doubt 'tis true, but only a Visus can see them outside the walls of the Ash Tree. All that can be done now is to wait, boy."

~

While Cyrano was escaping with Ambrose, Dooley had searched and found Birna's secret room. It took Dooley the better part of an hour of failed attempts to remember the incantation, but he had finally said, "*Fitlay, Breegla, Heert…Leeday, Jorgna, Kreet!*" The eyes of the woman in the painting and the medallion had glowed, and the wall had slid aside.

Now in the room, Dooley was overwhelmed with what to do. The room was empty except for a deep well surrounded by a ring of stones. The inside of the well was endless gray-blue. A swirling, cool wind spiraled up from the well, whipping Dooley's hair and clothes. Hovering above the well about halfway up from the floor, was a floating blue orb about as big as a tennis ball. It gave off the only light in the room.

Dooley walked from the ceiling to the part of the wall closest to the swirling well. His face was bathed in an eerie, blue glow. Closing his eyes to concentrate, he searched for how to proceed. From memory, he explored Ambrose's journal for answers, but nothing came to mind.

Remembering the conversation between Olaf and Padda he had overheard about the secret room, Dooley decided he must destroy the magical orb in order to release Dúfa, Egill, and all the others from the curse, but how? Stretching his arm toward the well, he attempted to drag a finger through the stream of air buoying the orb. Instead of easily slipping under it, Dooley realized the air was actually attached to the orb like a string attached to a soaring kite.

He reached into his backpack and withdrew the pocketknife and the jelly jar. Dooley held the knife between his teeth while he opened the jar. Then he held the lid and knife with one hand and the empty jar with the other. In one swift motion, he cut through the invisible threads. Tiny icicles fell on his hand, melting instantly. As soon as it was cut, the orb began to float toward the ceiling, but Dooley trapped it in the upturned jar. Quickly, he screwed the lid on tightly. As soon as it was secure, the atmosphere in the room was entirely changed.

With a deafening *whoosh*, a violent gust of wind came roaring from the bottomless well, followed by a woman's voice: "Fool!" she screeched, "Thou shalt pay for this!" The wind began to churn and heat up until it was a fiery tornado bursting up from the well and spreading onto the ceiling. As Dooley made his way to the door, the walls began to heat up, and he realized the rubber soles of his shoes were melting and sticking to the wall's surface.

"Fitlay, Breegla, Heert…Leeday, Jorgna, Kreet!" Dooley screamed between coughs, nearly overcome by the heat of the room. The door slid open, but he couldn't move. His shoes were stuck to the wall. He returned the knife and jar to his backpack. Then he leaned down to remove his shoes. Just as he was about to slip out of them, most likely falling on the floor, Ambrose appeared on the flying carpet. "Jump on, quickly!"

Without hesitation, Dooley slipped out of his shoes and landed awkwardly on his stomach on the carpet. They flew out just as the door slid shut. Dooley looked back and saw the woman in the portrait glower furiously at him.

"Have you got it?" Ambrose asked.

"What?"

"The orb."

"Oh, yes. It's in my bag." Dooley could feel heat radiating all around them as they whizzed down one corridor after another.

Glancing at the map, Ambrose said, "I think everyone's out, except the unfortunate ones in the dungeon, of course. Now we must destroy it."

"Destroy the dungeon?"

"No, the orb. We must destroy it to rob Birna of her power and release the children."

"Who are you?" Dooley asked.

"Why, how rude of me! I should've introduced myself right off. Ambrose Eustace Sullivan, at your service."

Ambrose steered the carpet up the steep stairways, stopping just outside the entrance.

"Psst! Come hither!" a voice whispered gruffly. Sitting by the lever was a hound dog with the wooly head of a sheep. "'Tis I, Vígi."

"What is it, my wooly friend?" Ambrose asked.

"I wilt heave the lever to open this contraption that thou might flee from this destruction," Vígi answered.

"But how will you escape, Vígi?" Dooley asked. "The door will shut before you'll be able to get out."

"I wilt find a way, sir!" shouted Vígi.

"Stay, loyal pup!" Ambrose commanded him, "I've still a job to do, Vígi, but if I haven't returned and the heat gets to be too much for you, leave without me."

"What do you mean?" Dooley cried. "You have to come with me! I don't know how to destroy the orb!"

"The answer is in you, Dooley. You've been given a rare gift, and the true purpose of any gift is always for the ultimate blessing of others. I know this now…almost too late. In spite of my gift…our shared talent…I've been blind. Don't be as foolish as me, Dooley."

"But what if I can't do it?"

"Remember: 'Faith is to believe what you do not see. The reward of this faith is to see what you believe.' Saint Augustine said that—quite a quotable fellow, old Auggie. Now hop off onto that top step. No reason to worry about Birna discovering you now." They heard an explosion of burning and popping wood above them, followed by a crack of a branch falling on the ground outside. "She surely knows you're here."

Dooley obeyed and jumped onto the step. After a quick salute, Ambrose turned the rug around and flew down into the darkness of the stairs.

"I'm ready, Vígi!" Dooley shouted.

Vígi pulled back the lever with a strong paw and the door creaked open.

Dooley looked out the door and saw the Mulligans waiting for him on the other side. The sun was beginning to set behind them, casting the family in an orange glow. Dooley could mainly see just their silhouettes.

"Come on, Dooley!" Cyrano cheered. "You're almost out!"

Just as Dooley approached the doorway, he heard a whinnying from below him. He turned just in time to see a tall, slender woman, dressed in a white robe with flowing silver hair riding on a white horse.

"*Jorgna Kreet!*" she yelled, and the door slammed shut.

Chapter 26

THE BIRTHDAY GIFT

"Dooley!" Cyrano shouted. He ran to the tree and pounded on the closed door with both fists. "Dooley!"

"'Tis Birna's doing, make no mistake of that," growled Homer.

"What can we do?" Cyrano asked him. "It's nearly sunset. Dooley will be trapped!"

"Celeste, love," Callidora said to her youngest daughter. "I think it's time for you to open your present."

"Mom!" Cyrano exclaimed, fighting tears. "How can you think of birthday presents at a time like this?"

Callidora ignored him and held Celeste's face in her hands. Then she removed Celeste's glasses and traced her finger along the constellation-like freckles on either side of her nose.

"'He determines the number of the stars and calls them each by name,'" Callidora quoted. "'When I consider your heavens, the work of your fingers, the moon and the stars, which you have set in place…' Yes, love, it's time."

"Mommy?" Celeste squeaked.

"You are a Caelum. Your gift is to…"

"…To stop the stars," Celeste finished her sentence. "But how long can I hold off the night?"

"Long enough, I hope," answered Callidora. "We've got to give Dooley more time." She returned Celeste's glasses to her face and stepped back.

Celeste closed her eyes and raised her hands up toward the sky. Following a few minutes of concentration, every-thing—the clouds, the birds, even the tiniest ants—stopped and held its breath.

~

"Thou art the traitorous fiend who hast destroyed my fortress!" Birna had grabbed Dooley and thrown him across her lap like a naughty toddler. "Thou shalt pay dearly for thy crime." Her words echoed in Dooley's ears as her horse pawed impatiently on the steps. "*Weert-troomba!*" Birna said, looking up at the ceiling. A passageway appeared above them and the winged horse flew up through the hole. Vígi cowered, unnoticed, in the shadows.

Dooley struggled on his stomach while Birna kept one hand pressed on top of his back. Eventually, he was able to roll over and sit up. As Birna continued to berate him, Dooley stealthily removed the jar from his backpack and wrapped it inside the folds of his sweater.

"These art mine children. They were pledged to me by

their slow-witted father. I am their mother; the only mother they have known for nearly a thousand years, but they do not heed my words. They do not appreciate that which I have given them. I shalt see them all destroyed!" Dooley shivered at the high pitch of her shrill voice.

After several minutes of flying higher and higher inside the trunk, they burst through burning leaves and branches to coast above the very top of tree, almost seventy feet high. Birna's horse flapped its wings nervously, unsure if it should alight on a branch or stay aloft. "Look down at what thou hast caused, stupid boy." Her large hand gripped the back of Dooley's head and tilted it down so that he could see the Mulligans on the ground.

Olaf's children gathered in groups of fives and tens, huddled together uncertainly. "When the sun has set, all of mine children foolish enough to disobey me and remain outside shalt be extinguished in a blue flame of searing pain and suffering." Dooley turned to look at Birna's face. He was haunted by her expression. He saw no remorse for the unfortunate turn of events, only joy in the coming punishment.

As the minutes passed by, the flames of the tree licked at the horse's wings, forcing it to snort and kick. Birna screamed, "Why is the day still here? The moon is late! Fear not, vile worm! Thou shalt die, nonetheless, but not before you see mine children die first. Mine horse fears these flames so we shalt leave our perch to find another viewing place."

She steered her horse back through the passages and

secret trapdoors until they reached Olaf's chambers. Smoke was beginning to fill the room. Though it had no effect on Birna, Dooley was choking, barely able to breathe. She pushed him off her horse, and he landed with a thud on all fours. "Aha!" she said as she wrenched his backpack from him. Birna unzipped it and rifled through it.

"It's not in there," Dooley said. "I dropped your magic tennis ball thing in the hallway," he lied.

She glared at him with narrowed eyes and continued searching. Moments later, Birna withdrew Ambrose's journal. When she flipped through it, her face was filled with rage. "I should have known that wretch wast behind this! If only I had killed him when he was still a whimpering boy!"

She touched the backpack with the long, red nail on her forefinger and threw the bag up in the air. It caught fire and burned up instantly. The ashes wafted down to the floor. Dooley fell to his knees and bent over them, forcing himself to comprehend any chance of escape was lost with the journal and compass. He sifted his fingers through the ashes.

Dooley stood, his knees shaking and tears running down his cheeks. "Go ahead. Kill me."

"'Twill be my pleasure," she sneered.

"But first, tell me," Dooley started, "what would've happened if we had won…if we had destroyed your magical orb before sunset?"

"Foolish boy," Birna said, as she ran a pointed fingernail along his cheek and down his chin, "I shalt never be defeated."

"But if you were…"

"I wouldst be banished from this world…"

A burning beam from the ceiling landed with a crash on the floor between them, and Dooley fell back on the couch. In the confusion, he pulled the jar from his sweater pouch.

He twisted off the lid and the orb floated up. Just as it left the jar, Dooley grabbed the orb and held it with both hands. The glass jar shattered where it fell. A burning sensation of extreme hot and extreme cold pulsed through his fingers. The pain was almost unbearable, but he closed his eyes and began: "Be brave…"

"My light!" Birna screamed. "Give it to me!"

"Shockwave…must save the enslaved…"

"Stop that!"

"Love's light makes right."

"Silence, fool!"

"The good fight needs sight."

Dooley opened his eyes and saw Birna stumbling towards him. She stepped over the burning beam, her horse behind her snorting frightfully with wide eyes. As Birna stretched her right arm out to grab him, her hand disappeared. She reached with her other arm but stopped when she saw her left hand had vanished, too.

"Be brave," Dooley repeated, with added confidence. "Shockwave…must save the enslaved. Love's light makes right…"

"No!"

"The good fight needs sight."

With a loud, bright blue explosion, Birna and her horse disappeared. Dooley let go of the glowing orb. He watched as it floated up. When it reached the ceiling, it popped like a harmless bubble and was gone.

Dooley staggered out of Olaf's chambers and hesitated. He knew he'd never be able to navigate the maze of the hallways without the enchanted compass. Smoke poured into the corridors. With painful, singed fingers, Dooley tugged his bandana over his mouth and nose. He ran down one hallway, but it only led to a dead end. Dooley leaned against a wall but pulled away quickly, feeling the heat on the other side.

Fighting hopelessness, Dooley suddenly thought of Ambrose's final words to him: *You've been given a rare gift*.

"Yes," Dooley said, "The gift of sight." He pulled his bandana so that his eyes were covered. "Faith is believing what you don't see." Starting with a walk that turned into a run, Dooley began to find his way out.

Chapter 27

A FOND FAREWELL

Celeste's arms were shaking terribly, and her pale face was tinged with green. She couldn't hold out anymore. "No! Please!" she cried as she fell to the ground. The sun dipped down into the field. The pink and orange streaks were replaced with a deep, dense cobalt blue. Celeste wept into her hands. "I couldn't do it," she sobbed. "I just couldn't." Callidora and Lloyd went to their daughter, rocking her and stroking her hair to comfort her.

"You did your best, love," Callidora whispered, "and no less."

With a crash, the door to the tree opened, and a pile of people flew out. The scorched and fraying carpet that held them drifted to the ground slowly as if it was aware of the fragile condition of its occupants.

"Dooley!" Cyrano exclaimed as soon as he saw his friend. Dooley rolled off the carpet, his arms and legs spread out.

Clio gasped when she saw his burnt and blistering fingers.

"Cashel," Lloyd called to his oldest son, "Go and get Dooley's parents. He's hurt badly, I'm afraid."

Cashel ran away from the field in the direction of Dooley's house.

Along with Dooley, the family saw Ambrose, Olaf, and two other young men. Ambrose alone remained on the carpet. The edges curled in to hug him as Ambrose drew in ragged breaths with great difficulty. He tried to sit up and sputtered, "Dooley…where is he?"

"He's here," said Granny, tears spilling down her wrinkled cheeks. She knelt beside him. "You all made it out." She lifted his head, so it could rest on her lap.

"He saved us," one of the young men murmured, "from the dungeon…I thought all was lost…"

Ambrose looked into Granny's face, his pupils contracting and dilating as he tried to focus. "Dorothea…could it be?"

"Daddy!" Granny cried. "But how could you know me after all these years?"

"You forget, my dear girl, my eyes see what others cannot. I see the little girl who still lives inside of you." Ambrose coughed and fought for breath.

"Oh, daddy…"

"I'm sorry, Dorothea."

"Hush, now."

"But I just couldn't leave them down there." Cyrano, Clio, and Cicely hovered over Dooley's motionless body.

"I ask this question full of dread: Is Dooley alive or is he dead?" Clio inquired.

"He's breathing," answered Cyrano, as he watched Dooley's chest rise and fall, "but he doesn't look good."

Cicely pulled out her harmonica and began to play. The tune was similar to the one she had taught Dooley how to play on the recorder, a simple combination of four notes. After running through it a few times, she dropped the harmonica in her lap and started to sing. The tune was the same. There were no words, only sounds. Everyone sitting in the dark, quiet field heard the song and saw a picture of home.

In his mind, Dooley saw his parents and his new best friend Cyrano. He saw their house and the wild, weedy field out front.

Olaf saw a hovel, nothing more than a mud hut. He was tending a fire outside. His father, red-bearded with a fur cape draped across his shoulders, was just coming home from hunting with a deer slung across his broad back.

The young men on either side of him saw their mother calling them to dinner. As they walked through the door, she lovingly swatted their backsides and fretted over their dirty hands.

Ambrose saw his wife Rebecca in her rocking chair by the fireplace, complex needlework in her lap. He saw Dorothea, five years old with long braids and big blue eyes. She sat on the floor by Rebecca's feet, winding yarn into a ball. Ambrose began to cough again, arching his back and digging his heels in the carpet.

After the coughing fit ended, he grabbed Granny's hand and smiled weakly, "Farewell, dear daughter. I'm gone to find your mother. She'll be wondering where I've been."

"Goodbye, Daddy." Granny bent to kiss his forehead and saw that he was dead. His face instantly lost the glow of the living. "Help me, please." She looked up at her family. "I want to move my daddy inside. It's time he found some rest."

Lloyd, Callidora, Calix and Crispin each picked up a corner of the carpet and carried Ambrose's body to their house. Granny, holding Celeste's hand, followed them inside.

"Padda, Vígi," Homer called to the young men on the ground, "Come here and stand with your kinfolk."

The young men stood and looked around them in wonder. Forming a ring around Dooley were nearly fifty people dressed in plain homespun clothes. The oldest man had a wooden leg and looked to be in his late thirties. He adjusted a leather satchel hanging across his chest. The oldest woman had long red hair with a wide, white streak starting at her crown. She cocked her head and smiled softly. The younger members of the group were men and women in their twenties.

Olaf stood and regarded his family with a mixture of trepidation and pride. "Mine children," he said. "After all these years, we have escaped."

Homer hobbled over to Olaf and poked him in the stomach with his cane. "Thou art no father. Thou art a selfish oaf."

"How dare you..." Olaf began.

"And we shalt not be bothered by the likes of you again." As Dúfa took his arm, Homer turned his back to Olaf. "Come, mine brothers and sisters. There is room enough for all in mine house. 'Tis the miracle I have dreamed of all these years." Dúfa kissed him on the cheek and they led the way past Dooley's house to the back fields and Homer's cabin.

Olaf skulked behind them at the end of their processional hoping for a handout and a bedroll.

After a few steps, Egill turned around and walked back to the spot where Dooley lay. He opened his satchel and pulled out a wooden figurine, the stacking doll from Dooley's house. Egill tossed it to Dooley. Before joining his brothers and sisters, Egill saluted him.

Chapter 28

SUMMER VACATION

When Dooley's parents, Paul and Rose, finally arrived in the field, they were out of breath and pale with worry.

"Dooley!" his mother said, rushing to his side. By now, Dooley was sitting up and looking at his restored fingers, the beneficiaries of Cicely's healing song. "Are you okay, sweetie?"

"I'm fine…really," Dooley answered.

Dooley's father whistled. "What happened to that big tree?"

He was surveying the scorched dirt and grass where the tree formerly stood.

"It caught fire," said Cyrano.

"We've been at the movies," said Rose, "Was there a thunderstorm? It looks like the tree was struck by lightning."

"But where are all the branches?" Paul asked. "That tree was huge. It couldn't have burned long enough to be completely reduced to ashes."

"Yeah, weird, huh?" said Dooley. "Anyway…we're all fine, right guys?"

Cicely, Clio, Cashel, and Cyrano all nodded and replied in unison, "Uh-huh."

Just then Dooley looked down and saw the Egill-like creature rooting in dirt. Cyrano spotted it, too, and shifted to the right to hide the odd, hybrid animal.

"What is that?" Rose asked.

"What?" asked Dooley nervously. He wasn't prepared to explain his adventures to his parents yet.

"Is that my matryoshka doll?"

"Oh, yeah…I borrowed it."

"Oh, okay," said Rose as she helped Dooley stand up. "And speaking of things that belong in the living room…Dooley, do you know what happened to the picture grandma made that said HOME SWEET HOME on it? I was dusting the living room, and it's missing."

"And where is my tent?" asked Paul. "It wasn't in the garage."

"About those…Dad, Mom…I kinda lost them…" Dooley answered as truthfully as he could without going into too much detail. He didn't have the energy to tell his father his tent must have been burned when the tree caught fire.

"Dooley Creed, I'm surprised at you!" Rose was brushing off the back of Dooley's shorts when she noticed something in his pocket.

"What is this?" She pulled out the brass compass. The glass face was slightly cracked but it appeared intact.

"The compass! I thought it was in my backpack!" Dooley exclaimed.

"Your backpack?" asked Paul. "Where is your backpack?"

"Also lost," Dooley answered.

"Time to come inside, Son. You've got a lot of explaining to do," said Paul.

Cyrano walked with Dooley to his house before going home. "I'm glad you're alright, Dooley. I was really worried."

Dooley was looking down at the compass, watching the needle spin around lazily.

"Yeah, me too. Although, I don't know what I'll do the rest of the summer."

"What do you mean?"

They stopped just before climbing the steps to Dooley's front porch.

"Well, it's hard to imagine what to do the next six weeks of summer vacation. Nothing's going to top nearly dying while defeating a mythical Valkyrie and rescuing an enchanted family from a curse."

"True."

"If only there were more people like us," Dooley leaned in to whisper, "you know, with powers."

"Sure there are."

"There are?"

"Of course. We meet all kinds at summer camp every year." Cyrano patted him on the back. "Well, good night, Dooley!"

Just before climbing up his front steps, Dooley stopped to

watch his friend as he walked away. About halfway between their houses, Cyrano stopped to observe something rustling in the grass of his dark yard. He called, "Here, kitty-kitty!" He bent down and scooped up the dove/cat and ran the rest of the way to his house. As soon as he opened the door, Cyrano yelled, "Mom, can I have a pet?"

Dooley smiled as he glanced back down at the compass, still spinning and waiting for Dooley to decide where he wanted to go next. He slipped it carefully into his back pocket, delighted to know the compass—a tangible piece of the adventure from the last two weeks—still existed.

He opened the front door and called, "Hey, Mom! Can I go to summer camp with Cyrano?"

ABOUT THE AUTHOR

Abby Rosser makes her home in Murfreesboro, Tennessee with her husband and four kids. She enjoys reading, watching movies, baking (and eating) desserts and being outside...but not all at the same time.

And she loves imagining stories (often when's she's doing most of the above).

Find out more about Abby at abbyrosser.com.

CPSIA information can be obtained
at www.ICGtesting.com
Printed in the USA
BVOW09s1218281217
503831BV00001B/8/P